"I love April," Eugenia sighed

The calm expression on Gerard Grenfell's face didn't alter. "I must agree, but I think I'll wait for May."

She studied him, puzzled. "Why do you say that?"

He started the car. "Somebody—Edward Way Teale, I think—wrote, 'All things seem possible in May.'"

"Oh." She was just as puzzled. "Do you plan to get married then?"

He said gravely, "You take the words from my mouth, Eugenia."

She felt vaguely depressed. Gerard's choice of a wife was his own business, of course, but she couldn't help believing that if he married Miriam he would be making the mistake of a lifetime. It was a pity she didn't know him well enough to tell him so.

Books by Betty Neels

These books may be available at your local bookseller.

Don't miss any of our special offers. Write to us at the following address for information on our newest releases.

Harlequin Reader Service
P.O. Box 52040, Phoenix, AZ 85072-2040
Canadian address: P.O. Box 2800, Postal Station A,
5170 Yonge St., Willowdale, Ont. M2N 6J3

Heidelberg Wedding

Betty Neels

Harlequin Books

TORONTO • NEW YORK • LONDON
AMSTERDAM • PARIS • SYDNEY • HAMBURG
STOCKHOLM • ATHENS • TOKYO • MILAN

Original hardcover edition published in 1984
by Mills & Boon Limited

ISBN 0-373-02680-3

Harlequin Romance first edition March 1985

CHAPTER ONE

A CHURCH clock somewhere close to the hospital struck the hour and Sister Eugenia Smith sighed, put down her pen, gave her muslin cap an unnecessary twitch and got to her feet, to walk, as she had done on so many previous occasions, out of her office and into the ward. She went unhurriedly, casting an eye here and there as she passed, to make sure that everything was just so, and came to a halt by Staff Nurse Bristow, waiting with her bundle of charts under one arm while one of the student nurses hovered with a trolley, equipped with all the odds and ends which might be required on the round. Eugenia smiled widely at her right hand as she joined her. 'One day,' she said softly, 'I shall leave the office a few seconds late and Mr Grenfell will arrive a few seconds early—that'll make history!'

She composed her features into a suitable seriousness as the swing doors were pushed open and the Senior Consultant Surgeon strode through them, ready to make his weeky round. Hatty Bristow, watching him greet Sister Smith with impersonal courtesy, wondered for the hundredth time how it was possible for the pair of them to be so indifferent to each other, for they were surely meant to fall in love at first sight; Mr Grenfell, with his tremendous height and size, his lint-fair hair and sleepy blue eyes, and Sister Smith, dark-haired, dark-eyed and lovely to look at—a tall girl, generously built. Hatty, mousey-haired and flat-chested, envied her from the bottom of a loyal heart. She considered that Eugenia was throwing herself away on Humphrey

5

Parsons, the Medical Registrar at St Clare's, although he was a good-looking young man, clever at his work and with a charm she had never trusted—but then he had never bothered himself over her; she was a plain girl and shy, and she was ready to admit that perhaps that was why she didn't like Sister Smith being engaged to him. And as for Mr Grenfell, he was engaged too—to a beanpole of a blonde, beautifully made up and dressed, who had come to the ward at Christmas and ignored everyone. Not nearly good enough for him, Hatty had decided. She sighed, a shade too loudly so that Mr Grenfell looked at her, and when she went red, smiled nicely and wished her a good morning before turning to Sister Smith.

His polite: 'Shall we start, Sister?' received an equally polite: 'Certainly, sir,' and she led the way to the first bed, followed by Mr Grenfell, his registrar, his house surgeon, Hatty Bristow, the lady social worker, in case Mr Grenfell should require her services, and hovering on the perimeter, Nurse Sims and her trolley.

It was a small ward, only twelve beds, none of them ever empty for more than a few hours, for the waiting list was a long one, and although St Clare's was an old hospital, the chest unit was modern, well equipped and meticulously run by Eugenia. She had taken over the ward three years ago from Sister Atkins, a dear old thing thankful to retire from the modern world of a profession suddenly full of technology which she had never quite understood. Eugenia had realised at once that Mr Grenfell was brimming over with new ideas and spent the first enthusiastic six months carrying them out, marvelling the while that he had never so much as hinted to Sister Atkins that he had them in mind. By the end of that time, the ward had been modernised, equipped with the very latest of surgical aids, and ready to admit the steady flow of patients in Mr Grenfell's care.

And he had achieved the same results with the men's ward at the opposite end of the wing, getting exactly what he wanted with a calm determination which never admitted of defeat, and always very pleasantly. Eugenia couldn't remember ever seeing him in a really nasty temper; true, if something had gone badly wrong, his handsome face became a mask of blandness and his voice, never loud, became a deeper rumble. But he had never told anyone off in the ward, waiting to do that in decent privacy, although she had never been a witness of such a happening. By all accounts, though, a few short sentences from him were far more effective than the occasional loud-voiced complaints of some lesser men. Indeed, she had seen some luckless student standing quite unabashed while a senior man ticked him off in front of his companions, and that same student, requested in Mr Grenfell's quiet voice to see him in his office later, turn as white as his coat, so that she had felt compelled to fortify him with strong coffee before he obeyed the summons.

Now, after three years, she knew exactly what Mr Grenfell liked, and being a good nurse, endeavoured to give it to him; punctuality to the second, short, factual answers to his questions, and a devotion to her work which ignored the clock on occasions. Not that she didn't rebel against these at times, especially when Humphrey had arranged an evening out together which had to be curtailed or even abandoned altogether because an emergency had been admitted or a patient had had a relapse ... Humphrey tended to be a little impatient on these occasions, and, for that matter, so did she.

Eugenia took the first of the charts from Hatty's

hand, gave Mr Grenfell the board from the end of Mrs Dunn's bed and took up her station opposite him. Mrs Dunn, a cheerful cockney who had lived within a stone's throw of the hospital for most of her life, had been operated upon two days previously for what she described as 'a nasty old chest', and which Mr Grenfell, out of her hearing, referred to as pyothorax, brought about by a sketchy convalescence from pneumonia and several wasted months of sampling every cough and cold remedy on the chemist's shelves.

Mr Grenfell sat himself down in comfort on the side of her bed, blandly disregarding Eugenia's faint frown and well aware that no one other than himself would dare to do so. 'How's the chest?' he wanted to know.

Mrs Dunn summoned a smile. 'So-so, and don't go telling me what you've done, because I don't want ter know, see? When I'm on my feet, that's time enough. And I'll thank yer ter take out that tube that's hanging over the bed . . .'

'All in good time, Mrs Dunn. Sister shall take it out for you tomorrow. It's doing a good job of work there, so bear with it.'

Mrs Dunn snorted weakly. 'I won't say 'as 'ow yer not pretty 'ot stuff at yer job, Sister too, though what a pretty thing like 'er's doing in this dump beats me!'

Mr Grenfell turned to look at Eugenia, studying her through half closed eyes. 'Yes, she is pretty, isn't she?' he observed. 'She's also very good at her job, so just you do as she tells you.' He got up, took the chart from Eugenia's hand and read it, scribbled a line or two and handed it back. Their eyes met for a moment, pleasantly indifferent to each other.

The next three patients were within a day or so of going home, so beyond a brief examination of them, and a few instructions to Harry Parker, his Registrar,

Mr Grenfell didn't linger, but the next case, a teenager with chest stab wounds, took up a good deal of his time. The girl wasn't doing as well as she should. Without speaking, Eugenia handed him the chart and pointed unobtrusively to the raised pulse and temperature. Mr Grenfell frowned. 'Antibiotics?' He then looked at Harry.

They weren't doing much good, indeed they had been changed twice.

'I'll take a look, Sister,' said Mr Grenfell, and waited while curtains were drawn, the trolley wheeled nearer and the patient got ready. The wounds were small, but then stab wounds always were, almost not to be seen. There was nothing wrong as far as could be seen, so he left Eugenia to make the girl comfortable and wandered off down the middle of the ward with Harry and the house surgeon. On the way to the next patient he paused to say to Eugenia: 'I'll have that girl back in theatre this afternoon, Sister, two o'clock. Usual pre-op treatment and Harry will write up the pre-med. There's some sepsis there and I'll have to look for it. Don't tell her until you have to.' He ruffled through the chart he was still holding. 'She's over eighteen? What about a consent form?'

'No, she's fifteen, but I've got her mother's phone number—I'll ask her to come right away.' Her lovely eyes studied his calm face. 'What shall I tell her?'

'I'll see her if you like. Try and get her here by one-thirty, will you?'

Eugenia nodded and they made their way to the next bed, its occupant a sprightly eighty-year-old with fractured ribs and lacerations of the lung. She had been admitted during the night and the lengthy business of examination began. Harry had already seen her, of course, but it was left to Mr Grenfell to decide what to do for her. Eugenia, anxious to get the patients' dinners served, thought him tiresomely slow; they were barely halfway round the ward. Her mind ran on ahead of her, reviewing the day. There was the girl for theatre, a handful of patients for X-ray and physiotherapy, patients to be got up and put to bed again, teas, medicines and a pile of tiresome little chores to do in the office. And she was off at five. Humphrey was off too, and they were going to spend the evening together; rather a special evening—dinner and dancing, in celebration of Humphrey's birthday. She began to be aware that Mr Grenfell was looking at her and went faintly pink, feeling guilty because her attention most unforgivably had wandered.

He didn't say anything, which made her feel even guiltier, but gave her some fresh instructions about the old lady's treatment and passed on to the next bed; a straightforward chest surgery, going along nicely. Eugenia recieved directions about discontinuing the drainage, removing tubes and getting the patient on her feet and waited for Mr Grenfell to inspect the next patient; she knew him well enough by now to recognise that this was one of the days when he wasn't to be hurried, and since she liked him in a vague impersonal way, she made no effort to urge him on. There was a faint smell of fish and soup coming from the ward kitchen, and her generous mouth twitched into a tiny smile as she saw his nostrils flare, but it made no difference to his rate of progress; he finished the round without hurrying, and at her pleasant: 'You'll have coffee, sir?' thanked her mildly and followed her into the office. She had time to hiss instructions about dinners to the attendant Hatty before she went past him and sat down at her desk.

Harry came with them, and the house surgeon, but

there wasn't room for anyone else. Mr Grenfell bade the lady social worker a polite goodbye, adding the rider that he would see her presently on the men's side, then he sat himself on the edge of Eugenia's desk. 'I'll be bringing half a dozen students with me on Friday afternoon,' he told her. 'The round will be rather longer than my usual one, I'm afraid. You'll be on duty?'

She had arranged to leave after lunch because Humphrey was free and it was an opportunity for them to browse round Selfridges pricing cookers, electric irons, kitchen equipment and so on. Humphrey intended to start married life with his home properly furnished down to the last pepperpot; a praiseworthy ambition which unfortunately meant that marriage was out of the question until they had saved enough money between them to achieve his wish. Eugenia, when they were first engaged, had declared that she really didn't mind if they had no stair carpet and odd tea-cups, but Humphrey wouldn't hear of it; he came from a solid middle class home, where everything matched, was polished and had its allotted place in a pristine household. And since his father had died, it had become even more pristine, so that Eugenia, when she visited her future mother-in-law, found herself plumping up cushions if she had leaned against them. If Humphrey had smoked she would probably have emptied the ashtrays as well, but he held strong views about the dangers of tobacco. Views not shared by Mr Grenfell, who with a careless: 'May I?' had taken out his pipe and was busy filling it while she poured the coffee.

She said with a briskness to disguise her disappointment: 'Yes, sir, I'll be here. Will you want anything special? And any particular patients?'

'Oh, Mrs Dunn for a start—she's so cheerfully unaware of her condition that she'll make a complete recovery.' He named several more and added: 'There will be two new patients tomorrow morning—I saw them in O.P.D. this morning. I don't think there's much we can do for either of them, but I'll see what can be done.' He turned to Harry and gave him instructions and then sat puffing at his pipe and drinking his coffee. He took up a good deal of space on the desk, and Eugenia thought vexedly that her neat piles of papers would be a fine muddle. Being engaged to Humphrey had turned her into a tidy girl. Sure enough, presently Mr Grenfell got up, spilling X-ray forms, diet sheets and off-duty lists all over the floor. He got down to pick them up, bundling them up any old how and putting them back on the desk so carelessly that some of them fell down again. 'Sorry, Sister,' he said mildly.

'It's of no consequence,' said Eugenia frostily, and was quite taken aback when he observed: 'You're quite right, it isn't. One can be too tidy, it makes for a warped way of living.'

A remark which left her unable to think of a suitable reply. She accompanied him to the ward door, bade him a civil good morning and watched him meander away, with his two companions, already late for his round in the men's ward on the other side of the corridor. Just for a few seconds she wondered what kind of a private life he had, and then forgot the thought, already busy planning the afternoon's work— she would have to spare a nurse to go to theatre and pray heaven Mr Grenfell made a quick job of whatever he intended to do.

It was unfortunate that he did no such thing, although she had to admit that his meticulous surgery had probably saved the girl's life. It had taken a good deal of exploration to discover the source of the sepsis and still longer to put it right. The girl had gone to the recovery room and then returned to the ward well after four o'clock. Eugenia hadn't got off duty until almost six, because however much she wanted to, she couldn't leave the ward until she was sure that the girl was going to be all right. Hatty was a splendid nurse, but Eugenia had always held the notion that the more senior you were, the more you had to be prepared to give up off-duty if the need arose. It wouldn't be fair to Hatty to leave her with an ill patient, the rest of the ward to run, the report to write and the nurses to manage. Even when she at last felt justified in going, she had walked slap into Mr Grenfell coming up the stairs two at a time. Naturally, he had stopped to ask her about her patient and she had stood for another ten minutes, listening carefully to his observations on the case. She even offered to go back with him to the ward, but he refused this with a cheerful: 'Hatty's there, isn't she? A sound young woman. I'll let Harry know if there's anything to be altered. Have a pleasant evening.'

He had gone, disappearing down the corridor at the head of the stairs at a great rate.

By the time she had run a bath, decided which dress to wear and done her nails, it was very nearly time to meet Humphrey. She wasted a few minutes inspecting herself in the wardrobe mirror; last year's dress was still quite wearable, but anyone with an eye to fashion would know that it was just that. A new one would be nice, it would cheer up the bleak days of a cold March, but it wasn't necessary, as Humphrey had pointed out, they wouldn't be going to any dances now that the spate of hospital balls and Christmas festivities were behind them, far better for her to save the money. And she had saved it, because, after all, he had been quite right, only somewhere at the back of her mind was a rebellious wish to splash out on a new outfit, not something sensible, but high fashion, real silk or real wool, and not bothering to ask the price.

She gathered up her purse and her coat and put her evening slippers on, reflecting that she would be going home the following week; Humphrey would be on call and hospital-bound. She had a sudden longing to be home now, cooking supper for her father and Becky and Bruce, wrestling with their homework, and after they were in bed, sitting by the fire with Plum the cat on her lap, while her father told her of some rare book he'd picked up in the Charing Cross Road. She sighed soundlessly and flew down to the nurses' home entrance, anxious not to keep Humphrey waiting.

She was a few minutes late, a fact which he had pointed out to her gently as he kissed her and ushered her into the car. 'I daresay you've had a busy day,' he observed. 'I know I have.' He got in beside her and she turned her head and smiled at him. He was a good-looking man, dark-haired and as tall as she was, good at his job and at the age of thirty, fairly sure of a secure future. She had often wondered why he hadn't married sooner, but when she had got to know him better she could understand that security meant a lot to him, so that although he had had girl-friends in plenty he had never been serious with them, only with her, because she was older and sensible as well as very pretty. She had been glad he thought her pretty, but she wasn't sure about being sensible and she wasn't all that old; twenty-six was still quite a way off thirty ... It would be another two years before they could marry too, unless she could persuade him that fitted carpets and a three-piece suite could not compensate for those two lost years.

But she wasn't going to think about that now; they had the evening before them and she intended to enjoy every moment of it. It was, after all, an occasion; a thirtieth bithday was an important event and justified the spending of money, and they hadn't had an evening out like this one since ... She paused to think about that; so long ago that she couldn't remember what they had celebrated. She asked: 'When was the last time you splashed out like this, Humphrey?'

'Our engagement, eighteen months ago.'

She said: 'Oh,' uncertainly, and then: 'Perhaps the next time it'll be to celebrate our wedding.'

'That's hardly likely, darling.' Humphrey's voice was, as always, reasonable. 'Even if we had a quiet wedding, we would have a few guests, I imagine, there'd be no point in celebrating twice over, would there?'

A sensible reply which for some reason annoyed her. 'Are we any nearer deciding the date?' she asked, and felt instantly mean at his quiet: 'Well, no, my dear, I only wish we were.' He gave her a quick sideways glance. 'I want to begin our married life together with as much comfort for you as I can manage.'

'Sorry—I didn't mean to be beastly. Only London gets me down at this time of the year. It's all right in the country—primroses and catkins and the first daffodils and lambs ... birds singing ...' She stopped because moaning in that self-pitying fashion was of no help to Humphrey—besides, never having lived in the country he wasn't all that interested. Memories of her home in Wiltshire came crowding back, but she pushed them away again; after all, her father and the twins seemed happy enough in the little terraced house in Islington; he was headmaster at a nearby school and Bruce and Becky were doing their 'O' Levels at the Upper School with every prospect of getting good passes. They seldom talked about Chidcoate Magna, and Eugenia hoped that in time they would integrate into the life of the city around them; something she had never been able to do.

They were going to the Savoy. Humphrey parked the
car and they went into the hotel, parking their coats
and meeting again in the foyer. 'This is fun,' whispered
Eugenia as they entered the restaurant and were led to
their table. She hoped they would have a drink and then
dance before they ate, but Humphrey pointed out that
both of them had had sketchy meals that day; dinner,
eaten at leisure, would do them more good. They could
dance afterwards for as long as she wished.

She sipped her sherry, her feet tapping soundlessly in
time to the music. Of course she was hungry, but she
longed to dance. The music came to an end and she
studied the menu. They were to have the set menu, for
as Humphrey had pointed out earlier on, the food was
so good it would be a treat anyway, and why pay
exorbitant prices when the same food, or almost the
same, could be had on the set menu. Eugenia agreed,
stifling the rebellious wish to order the most extravagant
dishes she could find. There must be something horrid
about me, she thought, I've done nothing but find fault
the whole evening. She blamed her day for that; and
that wasn't like her either, usually she took the days as
they came, some slack some so busy that there was only
time for a snatched cup of tea and a sandwich. Then she
thought longingly of her days off and catching
Humphrey's eye, wanted to make amends for her bad
mood. 'It looks gorgeous—I'll have the prawns, I think,
and then the chicken Marengo.'

After that she laid herself out to be a delightful
companion, listening to his considered opinions about
medicine, the National Health Service, the need to keep
up to date with his studies, his regret that he couldn't
see more of his widowed mother. Eugenia listened with
a sympathetic ear, although deep down inside her,
buried under her loyalty to Humphrey, was dislike of

that lady, a small frail person, with a wispy appearance which hid an obstinate wish to have her own way whenever possible. She lived very comfortably in a nice little house in Hampstead, and whenever they went to see her, she complained in the gentlest possible manner that it was just too far from St Clare's for Humphrey to go home each day. 'But of course,' she had observed in a sad voice, 'his career must come first—you'll remember that when you're married, I hope, Eugenia.'

Eugenia dismissed her future mother-in-law from her mind and attacked the prawns with relish, to have the edge taken off her appetite by Humphrey's: 'How splendid it would have been if Mother could have joined us.'

She smiled and agreed; he was a good son and she admired him for that. He would be a good husband too, she had no doubt, providing for her to the best of his ability, seeing that the children were decently educated ... She said warmly: 'I expect you're disappointed and I am sure she is, but her bridge evening does mean a lot to her, doesn't it? And this was the only evening we had free.'

He smiled at her and she thought again what a lucky girl she was to be loved by such a steady type. They ate their chicken talking comfortably and then got up to dance. The band was good and the floor not too crowded; Humphrey danced well even if without much imagination, and Eugenia had a chance to look around her. Her dress was definitely last year's—the creations whirling past, worn by slender creatures with exquisitely made up faces and up-to-the-minute hair-styles, showed it up for what it was. It was the wrong colour for a start, anyone who read the fashion magazines would see that at once, and it was too high in front and by rights should have almost no back. Eugenia, not needing to think about Humphrey's strictly conservative dancing, gave her mind to the vexed question of getting another dress. There was the Spring Ball in a few weeks' time, so there was every excuse to have one . . . on the other hand, if Humphrey could do without things in order to save for the future, so could she. She looked over his shoulder straight into Mr Grenfell's interested gaze.

He was with his fiancée; Eugenia recognised her at once, slim as a wand, not a hair out of place, perfect make-up and a dress such as she could never hope to possess. She gave him a cool smile and he opened his sleepy eyes and smiled back and then circled away. She noticed that he danced with the kind of nonchalant ease which reflected the way in which he did everything else.

Humphrey executed a correct turn. 'I see Mr Grenfell's here. That's a remarkably pretty girl—she's his fiancée, is she? I suppose she is. I must say he's taken his time, he must be thirty-five if he's a day.'

Eugenia said naughtily: 'Perhaps he's saving up . . .'

Humphrey's sense of humour wasn't quite a hundred per cent. 'Oh, certainly not that; he's very well off, I believe, one might say wealthy. Family money, you know.'

'No, I didn't know,' Eugenia told him, 'I've never been interested enough to think about it.'

He gave her hand a gentle squeeze. 'You're far too sensible a girl,' he observed approvingly.

And that from Humphrey was a compliment.

Mr Grenfell, Eugenia was quick to observe, was at a table for two not so very far from their own table. After discovering that, she took great care not to look in that direction again, and since Humphrey declared that he was too tired to dance again and had a hard day ahead of him they left very shortly afterwards. Eugenia would have liked to have stayed until the small hours, but

Humphrey needed his sleep, she knew that; his mother had explained at great length that unless he had his proper rest his health would suffer. She had stifled the remark that if that were the case, it would have been far better if he had never taken up medicine, a profession where sleep was sometimes sketchy to say the least, but she had agreed mildly, being a kind girl and wishing Mrs Parsons might like her and treat her as a daughter.

She got up at once and went to get her coat, and five minutes later was being driven back to St Clare's. And once there, their goodnights were swiftly said—not that Humphrey's kiss was not entirely satisfactory, but he showed no signs of lingering, only said briskly: 'Get to bed, dear—you need a good sleep and so do I.'

All the same, she tried to keep him for a few minutes longer.

'It was a lovely evening, Humphrey—I wish we could do it more often.'

'Now don't get ideas into your head!' He was half laughing at her. 'I'm not Grenfell, you know.' He added slowly: 'I must say his girl's a charmer. Not that you're so bad yourself—you could do with losing a few pounds, though. I'll work out a diet for you.' He patted her on a shoulder and got back into the car to take it round to the hospital garage, leaving her gibbering with rage. He had called her fat—not in so many words, but that was what he'd meant, and she wasn't—her weight was exactly right for her size and her curves were in all the right places. She went slowly through the hospital on the way to her room, feeling miserable. She wanted to please Humphrey, so she supposed she would go on to the diet, although she thought that for a young woman of her size, extreme slenderness would look all wrong; she was a big girl, walking proudly and unselfconsciously, but she had the frame to take a nicely rounded body, wouldn't she look silly if she were straight up and down, both back and front! She tumbled into bed and fell asleep with the problem unsolved.

She woke once in the night and remembered that she had forgotten to tell Humphrey that she wouldn't be able to get off on Friday afternoon—she must remember to tell him in the morning.

She saw him briefly just after breakfast. He looked very handsome in his white coat and grey suit, and well turned out, but then he always did; he considered it important that he should look his best at all times. Eugenia had just taken the report and was noting the day's work when he came down the ward and into her office, to give her a wry smile and say appreciatively, 'You look nice—very neat too. Uniform suits you, Eugenia.'

She pushed her work on one side. 'Compliments so early in the morning? You'll turn my head! Do you want to see someone?'

'Only you. I've written out a diet for you—you should lose at least half a stone in a month—it's easy enough to follow even on the hospital food.'

Eugenia cast a quick eye down his neat writing. Of course it was easy to follow; all she had to do, as far as she could see, was drink milkless tea and eat oranges and lettuce. 'Where's the protein?' she asked.

He leant over the desk. 'Here—fish and the odd ounce of cheese and a potato every other day.'

'I'll give it a whirl,' she told him. 'But if you get me on Women's Medical with anorexia nervosa, you'll be to blame.'

He laughed. 'You'll be a knockout! You'll have to take in the seams of your dress for the Spring Ball.'

She said seriously: 'Oh, no—I shall buy a new one.'

He frowned. 'That's absurd—a new dress for just one dance . . .'

Eugenia nodded her beautiful head briskly. 'That's right—and now I really must do some work.' She smiled enchantingly at him. 'And when I've given out the post I'll weigh myself.'

It was half an hour before she was back in the office. Giving out the morning's post was by way of being a social round as well; she had already been to see the ill patients and wished the ward a general good morning, but now she went slowly from bed to bed, handing out letters, listening to complaints, gossiping gently, taking care to stay a little longer with those who had no post that day, staying even longer by the beds of the ill patients, making sure that everything was just as it should be.

Harry would be round presently and there were several patients to go to X-ray, quite a few for physiotherapy and two to be got ready go home.

She sat down at the desk to check the operation list for the next day and check the list of admissions too. Besides that, she would have to rearrange the off-duty for Friday if Mr Grenfell intended to do a teaching round.

She was nibbling the end of her pen, frowning over this, when the door opened and Mr Grenfell walked in. 'I did knock, but you didn't hear,' he observed mildly. 'I'd like to take another look at that girl, if I may.'

He sat down on the edge of her desk and cast his eyes casually over its contents. Humphrey's diet sheet was still lying there and he picked it up.

'Good God, who's this for? A bit drastic, isn't it? I didn't know any of my patients were on a diet.' His eyes were suddenly frosty.

'They're not, sir, it's for me,' and at his enquiring look: 'Humphrey thinks I'm overweight . . .'

Mr Grenfell said strongly: 'Bunkum and balderdash, does he want you to fade away? You're perfectly all right as you are.'

Eugenia said seriously: 'Well, I'm the right weight for my size—you must have noticed that I'm—well, big.' She sighed. 'Most women these days are awfully slim, like wands.'

'So I've noticed.' He tore the diet sheet across and got up. 'You can tell your Humphrey what I've done. Now shall we take a look at this girl—Barbara, isn't she? Any news as yet as to who stabbed her?'

'None, sir, and she refused to say a word to anyone about it.'

He grunted deeply to himself, and when they reached the girl's bed, spent ten minutes there, joined by Harry, who had been warned that his chief was on the ward. Eugenia stood impassively while they examined Barbara, doing everything expected of her with a minimum of fuss. At length Mr Grenfell drew himself up to his great height. 'I think we're out of the wood.' He took Barbara's hand in his and smiled kindly at her. 'You're going to be all right, my dear, although you won't feel quite yourself for another few days. I'll see you again in a day or so, and Mr Parker will look after you, together with Sister.'

He turned away with Harry and at the ward door bade Eugenia a polite good morning in a remote manner, leaving her standing there with very mixed feelings. He had behaved in a most high-handed manner, tearing up her diet sheet in that fashion—and what was more vexing, she had had no chance to so much as protest. Truth to tell, he had seemed so different from his usual self that she hadn't quite known how to take him. Until now she had never taken a lot of notice of him; she had admired him as a surgeon, agreed with everything everyone said about his good looks, even felt a little sorry for him because he seemed, in her eyes, to be marrying the wrong kind of girl, but she had very seldom thought of him as anyone else but a surgeon for whom she worked. Indeed, she could hardly remember an occasion when he had discussed anything else with her but the condition of his patients. She found it vaguely unsettling.

It was a good thing that she didn't see Humphrey that day, for she hadn't made up her mind what to say to him; he was going to be put out, even angry, although he was never actually bad-tempered with her. All the same she shied away from having to tell him. And she still had to let him know that she wouldn't be free on Friday afternoon.

They met the next morning when she was on her way to X-ray and he was coming down from the Medical Wing. He said at once: 'How's the diet?' and smiled in a satisfied way.

'Well,' began Eugenia guiltily, 'I haven't started it yet, in fact I'm not going to—Mr Grenfell says . . .'

'What the hell has Grenfell got to do with it?' demanded Humphrey so sharply that she stared at him.

'I'll explain,' she said, and did so, making light of the whole thing.

'He had the nerve to tear my diet sheet up?' Humphrey usually so pleasant, looked like thunder, and she said smoothly:

'Well, it doesn't matter, does it? Such a little thing to fuss over . . .'

'I never fuss,' he reminded her coldly, 'and it's not a little thing——' He looked her magnificent person up and down. 'If you chose you could be as slim as that lovely girl he was dancing with.'

Eugenia caught her breath. Humphrey had never spoken to her like that before; even if he didn't mean it, and she was sure that he didn't, it hurt. At the same time it hardened her resolve to stick to her guns. She said quietly: 'Don't be silly, Humphrey. If you don't love me as I am, you know what to do.'

She turned on her heel and marched off down the corridor.

She was far too busy to give it another thought that day. An elderly woman with multiple chest injuries after a road accident came in before lunch, and needed to be got ready for an emergency operation, and when Mr Grenfell came to examine her, he was wholly concerned with his patient, and so for that matter was Eugenia. And there was a bewildered elderly husband to deal gently with. He drank cup after cup of tea, quite unable to take it all in. 'She was only popping down the road for the groceries,' he told Eugenia. 'She'll be all right, won't she?'

Eugenia comforted him and offered him a bed for the night, and phoned sons and daughters who ought to be told. 'If anyone can get her well, it'll be Mr Grenfell,' she assured him, and meant it.

The woman came back from theatre just before supper and Eugenia stayed for a while until the night nurses had got the other patients settled. By the time she got off duty it was too late to meet Humphrey; perhaps that was as well, she mused, going soft-footed through the Hospital towards the nurses' home; they'd be able to laugh together about the whole thing in the morning. She was in bed, half asleep, when she remembered that she had never told him that she wouldn't be free on the following afternoon.

CHAPTER TWO

IT was dinner time before Eugenia remembered with horror that she hadn't told Humphrey she wouldn't be off duty until the evening. She was halfway through her milk pudding when the thought struck her, and she leapt up from the table, to the surprise of her companions.

'I've just remembered,' she gabbled, and tore off to the porter's lodge, where she got old Belling to ring the Residents' flat. Humphrey's 'Yes?' was terse, and then: 'Oh, it's you—I'll be ready in half an hour.'

'Not me—I won't, Mr Grenfell's doing a teaching round and wants me on the ward . . .'

'At such short notice? I never . . .'

'It's my fault,' said Eugenia meekly. 'I forgot to tell you—he asked me a couple of days ago. You know he always insists on the Ward Sister being there when he's got students.'

'You forgot to tell me,' observed Humphrey nastily. 'Have I become so unimportant to you? First you ignore my special wishes for you to diet and now you ruin my half day!' Before she could speak, he added: 'I shall go home to Mother.'

It was quite unforgivable of Eugenia to giggle; the sound of the phone slammed down in her ear made her realise that. She went back to the ward, feeling guilty, incredibly mean, and at the same time vexed. Humphrey need not have been quite so cross about it—after all, it wasn't as if they were going to do anything special. Perhaps, she reflected, if they bought something from time to time, it would make their window-shopping more interesting. Her own nest-egg was piling up slowly in the bank, and she had no doubt that his was as well, but there was such a thing as inflation. By the time they actually married, probably they wouldn't be able to afford the things that he was so anxious that they should have.

Mr Grenfell, with a number of students trailing behind him, arrived, as usual exactly on time, and for the next hour or so she had no thought for anything but her work. Barbara was doing well now, so was Mrs Dunn, and so for that matter was the elderly lady with the chest injuries. He spent a long time with each of them, asking courteous questions of them and waiting, equally courteously, for the students to make observations. There was the usual know-all ready to answer everyone else's questions as well as his own, the usual slow thinker, who, given enough time, came up with the right answer and would probably in the course of time make an excellent surgeon. There were two women students today; both young and pretty and, Eugenia suspected, more interested in Mr Grenfell than the patients. He was good at getting the best out of them though, disregarding the know-all unless it was his turn, waiting patiently for the slower ones to give their answers, ignoring the two girls fluttering their eyelashes.

Eugenia, at her most professional, with Nurse Sims to back her up, took down dressings, sat patients up and laid them down again, whipped back bedclothes, adjusted drains and handed notes at the exact minute they were required, and doing all these things with a calm friendliness towards the patient so that the alarming sight of half a dozen strange people staring at the bed's occupant was tolerable after all. Unfortunately it was quite late by the time the round was over. She offered tea, but Mr Grenfell refused politely, dismissing his students with the observation that there were one or two notes he wanted to write. Eugenia led him to the office, handed over the charts he required and beat a retreat. As she reached the door he said quietly: 'You enjoyed yourself the other evening, Sister?'

She opened the door a little way, having no wish to discuss it with him. 'Yes, thank you, sir.'

'But you didn't stay long?'

'Well, no. Humphrey had a busy day ahead of him.' She thought as she said it that Mr Grenfell had had a busy day ahead of him too, but he had been dancing with every sign of enjoyment when they left.

'Ah, yes, of course,' said Mr Grenfell smoothly. 'You were celebrating? Your birthday, perhaps?'

'Not mine—his.'

She spoke sharply because he was looking at her unsmilingly, although she had the uneasy feeling that he was finding something amusing.

'Two safely engaged people, aren't we, Sister?' He sounded thoughtful. 'There is, of course, many a slip between the cup and the lip.'

'We've been engaged for eighteen months, sir.' She said it coldly.

'Indeed?' Just as though he didn't know. 'So you'll be marrying very soon?'

'In two years' time.'

'A long time to wait?' He raised his eyebrows.

'Humphrey—that is we, want everything bought and paid for before we marry.'

Mr Grenfell drew a large cat with handsome whiskers on her blotting pad. 'You do? Now that's something I can't understand.'

'I don't suppose you can,' said Eugenia tartly. 'I

daresay you have everything you could possibly need and are able to get married when you like.'

'Oh, indeed, yes.' He was quite unruffled by her crossness. 'But that doesn't mean to say that I shall.' He added a yachting cap and wellington boots to the cat, admired his handiwork and added a cigar. He looked up to smile at her. 'Don't let me keep you from your work, Sister.'

Eugenia flounced out of the office, rather pink in the cheeks. Mr Grenfell was excessively tiresome at times!

Somehow she didn't see Humphrey during the next day or two, she was off duty on the evening before her days off, and before she left the hospital she went along to the porter's lodge and asked to see him if he was available. It seemed that he wasn't; so she left a message, picked up her overnight bag and went to catch her bus. It was a pity she couldn't have seen him; occasionally he sulked, but she had always been able to get round him; she wasn't unduly worried, she had no doubt that when she got back to St Clare's everything would be smoothed over.

It was marvellous being home again. She was welcomed boisterously by the twins, invited to cook supper, and gently greeted with affection by her father. 'It seems a long time since you were home,' he commented vaguely.

'About ten days ago, Father. I quite often have to change my free days. And we've been busy.' She kissed the top of his head. 'Found any more books lately?'

Supper was delayed while he told her about a splendid copy of Milton's *Paradise Lost* which he had unearthed in some small, out-of-the-way bookshop.

Eugenia helped the twins with their homework after supper and then sat with her father in the cosy, shabby sitting room, discussing their future and ways and means; they were clever, the pair of them, bound to go to university, and the money would have to be found somehow. Even with grants there would be expenses. Eugenia said thoughtfully: 'Well, Father, Humphrey doesn't want to get married for at least two years; there's no reason why I shouldn't use some of the money I've saved to help out.'

Her father shook his head. 'My dear, Humphrey depends on those savings, I daresay.'

'Oh, he does, but we can wait another year—we shall have waited so long by then that I can't see that it will matter if there is a little delay.'

'It'll matter very much. It's not my business, Eugenia, but I can't agree with his ideas at all. You're both young and he has a good job—you could be quite happy in a small flat for a year or two. You could even go on working for a time.'

'Yes, I know, I've told him that, but he's set his heart on having just about everything before we marry. And then there's his mother . . .'

'What has she to do with it?'

'Well, she's not a very independent person, Father, she does depend on him quite a bit.'

Mr Smith made a derogatory sound. 'He's a grown man, a professional man, he has his own life—and your life—to lead, my dear.'

'Yes—well, I suspect it will all sort itself out.' She was suddenly weary; she seldom allowed herself to think too deeply about the future; Humphrey had told her so many times that he had it all sewn up and that she wasn't to worry, so she just let the months slide by— perhaps it needed something drastic to happen to jog them out of the rut they seemed to have got into . . .

It happened on the very morning that Eugenia returned to work. Mr Grenfell strolled into the ward, unexpected and unannounced, stood silently while she removed a chest tube and then followed her still silently down the ward to the sink, waited while she scrubbed her hands and then said: 'I want to talk to you, Sister Smith.'

Eugenia dried her hands and then led the way to the office. He probably wanted extra beds put up down the centre of the ward, or an emergency to be filtered into an already overflowing list. She sat herself down behind her desk, cast a lightning glance at the clock and asked politely: 'Yes, sir?'

'You may not know that from time to time I'm called into consultation in other countries. I've been asked if I'll examine, and if necessary operate on, the wife of a British diplomat in Lisbon. In actual fact they have a villa in the Algarve where she is at the present time. From what I hear from her doctor she has the signs and symptoms of a new growth of lung. If that's so then surgery is indicated, which I should carry out on the spot. It's required that I bring a nurse with me, conversant with the treatment of such a case, to see the patient through the first few days and demonstrate to a nurse there exactly what should be done. I should be obliged if you would accompany me, Sister. We should be away for a week if everything is satisfactory, ten days at the most, as I have commitments here. There's a small private hospital in the area where I should operate and where the patient will remain until she's convalescent. I imagine you're capable of demonstrating the post-operative treatment within two or three days, and you would, of course, return with me when I consider the patient to be out of danger.'

Eugenia had sat, her pretty mouth slightly agape, during this lengthy speech. After a moment of silence during which they looked at each other wordlessly, she said: 'When would you want to go, sir?'

'Two days' time, certainly no longer than that. A day sooner, if that could be arranged. I should like your answer now.'

'How long for? Ten days at the longest, you said . . .' She thought rapidly. She was to have spent her next days off with Humphrey's mother, who she felt sure would take it as a personal insult if anything should prevent that. On the other hand, it was her job—she was there to carry out Mr Grenfell's instructions, and this was, in effect, an order.

'What about the ward?' she asked.

There was a satisfied gleam in Mr Grenfell's half-closed eyes. 'I imagine Hatty could cope for a few days. Besides,' he continued with an entire lack of conceit, 'I shan't be operating, so it won't be all that busy.'

'Very well, I'll come with you, Mr Grenfell. Perhaps you'll let me know when exactly we're to leave and what I shall require to take with me. I do have a passport valid until the end of the year.'

'Good. I'll either see you this evening or send you a note.' He opened the door he had been leaning against. 'I'll arrange things with the Office,' he told her, and was gone before she could answer him.

Hatty had to be told, of course, and her father telephoned during her dinner hour. But she didn't say anything to anyone until she was summoned to the Office and given official permission to go with Mr Grenfell.

Over tea in the Sisters' room she mentioned it, aware that if she didn't the hospital grapevine would get hold of the news and pass it on, highly distorted.

'Whatever will that fiancée of his say to that?' demanded Chloe Watkins, who was in charge of the Men's Chest Unit on the other side of the landing. 'I wouldn't imagine she would take kindly to competition.'

'But I'm not competing,' offered Eugenia mildly, 'just doing a nursing job.'

'She won't believe that. You'll probably find her there as well, seeing fair play.'

Eugenia chuckled. 'We don't even like each other; I think Mr Grenfell's a super surgeon, and I supose he finds me adequate as a nurse. Besides, we're both going to be married . . .'

'Can't think why he waits so long,' said a voice, 'I mean, he's not exactly lacking this world's goods, is he?'

'Cold feet,' said someone else, and raised a laugh. And then: 'What will your Humphrey say, Eugenia?'

'I don't know—at least, he won't object. It's a job, like everything else, isn't it?'

'Well, I for one,' said that same voice, 'wouldn't mind going instead of you, Eugenia. Mr Grenfell is worth cultivating.'

'Well, if he is, I haven't got very far, and I've worked for him for three years now.' Eugenia got to her feet. 'I'm going back, there's still a case in theatre.'

The patient, an elderly woman with a stove-in chest, came back to the ward very shortly and Eugenia dealt with her needs with her usual calm. She had checked the two tubes and the blood transfusion, and made sure that the patient was as well as could be expected and was writing up the chart when Mr Grenfell came on to the ward. He spent a few minutes checking his patient's condition, nodded his satisfaction and asked Eugenia to go with him to her office. Eugenia finished her writing, whispered a few instructions to Nurse Sims, positioned by the bedside, and led the way down the ward.

'We go tomorrow evening by charter plane—five o'clock from here. I'll pick you up at the entrance. One small case, and take uniform. You can wear ordinary clothes for the flight, of course. Don't bother about money—I'll see to that, but remember your passport. We shall fly straight to the Algarve and be met at the airport, examine the patient during the evening and again in the morning, and if it's necessary arrange to operate that same day. You'll probably be very busy; not much time to sleep and no time off.' He started for the door. 'Anything else you want to know?'

Quite a bit, she thought, but as none of it was relevant to their actual journey there seemed little point in giving utterance to them. She said: 'No, I think not, sir,' and added, 'Goodnight,' and he nodded briefly and went.

Eugenia sat down again and made a list of what she would need to take with her. And then, of course, there was the question of telling Humphrey. He might be a bit sticky, she reflected, although he had no reason to be. All the same he would have to be told, and as soon as possible. She was off duty that evening, and he might be free for an hour or so; they might go to a pub for something in a basket instead of supper in the hospital.

Later that evening she had neither seen nor heard from him, so as she went off duty she went along to the porter's lodge and asked old Evans to find out where he was.

''ere yer are, Sister,' said Evans, and handed her the receiver.

Humphrey was free for the evening, and from the sound of his voice, still on the sulky side.

'A drink and a sandwich?' suggested Eugenia. 'I've got something to tell you.'

'Well, if it's important,' he agreed grudgingly.

They met an hour later in the entrance hall and she could see at once that he was still sulking. Her heart sank, and she spent the ten minutes' walk to the pub getting him into a good humour again. Over their chicken and chips in a basket and beer, she took heart and told him. The chicken and chips hadn't been enough; she watched him grow remote, sorry for himself and finally critical. 'I can't think why you have to go,' he observed coldly. 'There are plenty of other nurses—your staff nurse, for instance. What's so special about you?'

'Nothing, only I know his routine inside out and the nurse there will have to be shown what to do. Why are you making a fuss, Humphrey?'

He said with dignity: 'I am not in the habit of making a fuss, Eugenia. I merely remarked that I can't see the need for you to go. Have you accepted?'

'Yes,' said Eugenia calmly.

'Without consulting me?' He was definitely sulking again.

'Well, Humphrey, I didn't see the need for that. After all, I'm going on a nursing job, not a weekend at Brighton. And we're not married, you know.'

'We are engaged,' he reminded her, 'and I expect my wishes to be observed whenever possible.' He added, to make her quite savage, 'Mother wouldn't like it at all.'

Eugenia swallowed rage and hurt and annoyance. 'Humphrey, I'm sorry if you're annoyed about it—I never imagined you would be. And I can't think why.' She asked in a conciliatory voice: 'Don't you like Mr Grenfell?'

'That's beside the point,' said Humphrey loftily. 'You're going against my wishes.'

'How can I be doing that?' she asked reasonably. 'When Mr Grenfell asked me you didn't know anything about it.'

'You can at times be a very stubborn young woman,

Eugenia. However, we'll say nothing more about it. Presumably you'll be back in time to spend the weekend we'd arranged with Mother?'

Her heart sank at the very thought, but she said gently: 'Of course, dear. Mr Grenfell said a week, and our weekend is still a fortnight away.'

'I wouldn't want to disappoint Mother,' said Humphrey repressively. 'If you've finished, we might as well be getting back to St Clare's—I have a busy day ahead of me.'

'So have I,' said Eugenia, faintly waspish.

Sitting beside Mr Grenfell in his Turbo Bentley, being whisked towards Heathrow on the following afternoon, Eugenia wondered how on earth she had managed to be where she was. The ward had been extra busy, one of the part-time nurses hadn't turned up, Barbara had started running a temperature, and she had been at odds with the diet clerk as well as X-ray—not a good day, and she had gone off duty wishing she had never agreed to go with Mr Grenfell. She showered and changed, shut the one small case she was taking with her, checked her handbag for money and passport, and went down to the hospital entrance. He had been waiting for her, and after the briefest of greetings had put her case in the boot, ushered her into the front seat and got in beside her. And now here she was, a little edgy and tired, wishing she hadn't come. Humphrey had been right, as he so often was; she should have told him first before agreeing to go and taken his advice.

'Cold feet?' asked Mr Grenfell, hitting the nail on the head so accurately that she jumped.

'Yes. Humphrey didn't want me to come . . .'

He swooped past an articulated lorry. 'Why not?' He sounded interested, but only in a vague way.

'Well, I don't know—he didn't say.' She added thoughtfully: 'Perhaps because we're engaged . . .'

'I'm engaged,' observed Mr Grenfell carelessly, 'and as far as I know Miriam had no qualms.'

'Didn't you ask her?' Eugenia was curious.

'Certainly not. She has no interest in my work, indeed she finds it extremely boring.'

She had a momentary picture of him going home after a day's successful operating, bursting to tell someone about it, and not being able to say a word. Fleetingly she was sorry for him. She said carefully: 'Well, I daresay it's restful for you not to talk about your work when you get home.'

'Bunkum,' said Mr Grenfell. They were driving through the complexities of the airport now and a moment later he stopped outside Terminal Two. 'This is where we get out.'

There was a man waiting to take the car, presumably to garage it. Mr Grenfell picked up her case, handed his own and his case of instruments to a porter, and walked briskly into the booking hall. The formalities, which she had been rather dreading, took no time at all. She was ushered upstairs, told to sit down and not walk away until he returned. Which he did presently, with two cups of coffee and an armful of magazines and papers.

'About twenty minutes before our flight is called,' he told her, and opened *The Times*.

He didn't hurry when their flight was called, so that Eugenia became quite nervous about missing the plane altogether and longed to tell him to hurry up. They were some of the last to go on board, and she was secretly pleased that they were in the first class compartment. Not that she could see much difference between that and the rest of the plane, only it would sound so much better when she told everyone about it when she got back.

She didn't much care for flying, but since Mr Grenfell's impassive face betrayed no emotion whatsoever, she took care to sit very still, her insides knotted up, her hands clasped together on her lap.

'You can unwind now,' said Mr Grenfell laconically, 'we're airborne.' She had no intention of answering him, but gave him what she hoped was a cool smile and began on the pile of magazines, to be interrupted very shortly by the stewardess with food and drink. She wasn't particularly hungry, but it passed the time very nicely and made everything so normal that she peeped out of her window into the dusk below. It was quite a surprise when they were asked to fasten their seat-belts because they were about to land; it was even more surprising when Mr Grenfell, who had barely spoken throughout the flight, took her hand in one of his large firm ones, and held it comfortingly until they were safely on the ground.

They were met at the airport, and since there were not many passengers Customs formalities took only a few minutes. The Customs officer was young and dark and eyed Eugenia with appreciation as he asked Mr Grenfell why he was travelling. He went on looking at her while Mr Grenfell told him, but now his glance was tinged with respect. She heard the word *Medico*, and the man took another look at both their passports, said surprisingly: 'I wish you good luck, sir and madam,' and smilingly waved them both on.

The stout dark man who had met them picked up their bags and led them to where a large Cadillac was parked. 'One hour,' he said cheerfully, and swept Eugenia into the back seat while Mr Grenfell stowed his case, got in beside her and settled back in his corner. 'I shall take a nap,' he told her, and he did, while she tried to see where they were going in the almost dark.

Tantalising glimpses of villages with small houses bordering the road, signposts which she never quite managed to read as they tore past, and now and then the lights of villas standing back from the road. The car slowed and Mr Grenfell, sitting beside her, stirred. 'We're going to Portimao, I understand the house is just outside the town.' He yawned. 'I've never before met a girl who's so incurious—I find it so refreshing.'

Eugenia could see the lights of a town now and the glimmer of water. They crossed a bridge and drove along a wide boulevard with fishing boats crowding its edge, and the town on its other side. But they didn't stop, only drove on out of the town again, still with the river on their left, and after a while the car was turned into a narrow road and then into a drive overhung with trees. It opened on to a sweep before a house with lights shining from almost every window and the chauffeur got out, opened the car door and gestured from there for them to mount the steps and go through the open door. They had reached it when a man came hurrying towards them.

'Mr Grenfell? And your nurse.' He held out a hand. 'I'm Clarence—my wife's upstairs—in bed, of course. You have no idea how glad I am to see you! The doctor is with her now—we've had a bad day . . .'

He was a tall, thin, distinguished-looking man, and at the moment worried to death; as well he might be, thought Eugenia, shaking hands and then standing discreetly behind Mr Grenfell.

'You must be tired . . .' began Mr Clarence.

'Not in the least,' Mr Grenfell spoke for them both, and Eugenia felt indignation at his high-handedness. 'You would like us to see your wife as soon as possible, naturally. If we might have ten minutes to tidy up . . .?'

'Of course. The housekeeper has put you both on the

first floor, opposite each other, in case you need each other during the night.'

Eugenia heard Mr Grenfell mutter and chose to ignore it. She said calmly: 'I'll get into my uniform and be with you in ten minutes, Mr Grenfell.'

She was led away by a hovering maid, a pretty dark-haired girl dressed in black, to a room at the side of the house, nicely furnished with heavy dark bed, chest and dressing table, and with a shower room leading from it. Her case was already there; she fished out her uniform, spent five minutes in the bathroom and then got into her uniform and went downstairs again, very neat and fresh and looking reassuringly efficient.

Mr Grenfell looked at her from under heavy lids. 'Ah, yes. Do you speak any French?'

She opened her lovely eyes in surprise. 'A little— why?'

'Probably we may find it easier to talk in that language, the doctor and I.'

'I'll do my best,' she told him sedately, and followed him up the stairs behind Mr Clarence.

Mrs Clarence was in bed in a large room with a huge bay window draped extravagantly in brocade, a thick carpet underfoot and some massive dark furniture. She was a small, fair woman, quite lost in the big bed and very ill. She looked at them both with obvious relief as they went in, and so did the doctor with her. He went forward and shook Mr Grenfell's hand, and then Eugenia's. 'A pleasure to see you, Mr Grenfell,' he said in slow, correct English, 'and I know that my patient is just as pleased that you could come.'

Mr Grenfell went to the bed and took Mrs Clarence's hand. Eugenia admired his bedside manner before being introduced herself, then stood quietly while the two men exchanged a few words. Presently Mr Grenfell said: 'Dr da Marcos and I would like to have a short talk. Would you stay with Mrs Clarence, Sister Smith?'

So Eugenia drew up a chair and engaged her patient in gentle chat about nothing in particular. 'I feel better already,' declared Mrs Clarence, 'just seeing you sitting there in that nice uniform. My husband insisted on getting Mr Grenfell,' her eyes flickered towards Eugenia, 'he's quite certain that he can cure me.'

'He's a very good and famous surgeon,' said Eugenia. 'I'm sure he'll put things right.'

'He'll have to operate? Dr da Marcos said I had a bad infection of the lung.' She frowned. 'I don't want to go into hospital—they're not like hospitals at home, you know.'

'If you go, just for whatever tests and treatment Mr Grenfell wants you to have, I'll come with you, Mrs Clarence. And probably you'll be back here for your convalescence. Here they come back again; I expect Mr Grenfell will want to examine you and have a little chat.'

The examination took a long time, and when he had finished, he asked a great many questions. At length he said gently: 'I think it will be better for you if I operate, Mrs Clarence. Dr da Marcos has seen to all the arrangements, so there's no reason why we should delay. I'm going to take away part of your lung, and that means hospital for a day or two, but Sister will be with you and so will I, and you shall come home here within a few days. You'll be up on your feet within a week, feeling very much better. Suppose we say tomorrow afternoon? I'll make all the arrangements and Sister will know exactly what has to be done. Dr da Marcos is going to give you something to make you sleep, and I'll see you again in the morning.'

He went away with Dr da Marcos and left Eugenia to

make Mrs Clarence comfortable for the night, see that she took her pills and then sit quietly until Mrs Clarence dozed off.

It was getting late by now. Eugenia left a small lamp on in the room and went downstairs, where she found the three men sitting in the enormous living room, talking quietly. 'She's asleep?' asked Mr Clarence.

'Yes. I'll go and take another look presently. Is there a night nurse?'

'We had one, but my wife didn't like her—I sat with her last night, but now that you're here, she may sleep peacefully until the morning...'

'I shall want you in theatre tomorrow, Sister, so you must get a good night's sleep yourself. Perhaps there's someone reliable who would stay within call and rouse me if necessary?' Mr Grenfell sounded unworried, almost casual, but she knew better than to argue with him. There was a maid, an elderly woman, very trustworthy, said Mr Clarence; he would see to it, and in the meantime would they have the meal that was awaiting them?

Eugenia, quite sleepy by now, wasn't sure what she ate. It tasted delicious, though, and afterwards someone brought her a tray of tea, and when she had finished it, Mrs Clarence still asleep, Mr Grenfell said in a no-nonsense voice: 'Go to bed, Sister. If you're needed you'll be called. Be ready to take over at seven o'clock, will you?'

She said goodnight and went up to her room, had a quick shower and fell into her bed, to sleep at once, dreamlessly.

She awoke to a bright morning, with the sun shining from a blue sky. More like May than March, she thought, dressing quickly and going along to Mrs Clarence's room. The elderly woman who had spent the night there went thankfully away and Eugenia set about making her patient comfortable, so that by the time Mr Grenfell arrived at eight o'clock she was nicely propped up against her pillows and had drunk the tea which she was allowed to have. She had slept well too, and answered him cheerfully enough when he asked her if she was ready to go into hospital. 'This morning, I think,' he said kindly. 'There'll be several tests to do, and if they're satisfactory I'll operate this afternoon. We shall keep you there for a few days and Sister will nurse you, and at the same time there'll be a Portuguese nurse there whom she'll instruct, so that when we go you'll have exactly the same treatment.'

Mrs Clarence nodded. 'That's kind of you,' she said weakly. 'To tell you the truth, I feel so rotten I don't really mind what happens.'

'All the more reason to go ahead as quickly as we can,' said Mr Grenfell soothingly. 'I shall leave you with Sister Smith and very shortly an ambulance will take you in to Portimao.'

Eugenia was thankful that she hadn't unpacked her case; she was given barely ten minutes in which to collect her things together when the ambulance arrived and Mrs Clarence was loaded carefully into it. It was a low-slung vehicle with a blaring horn and a turn of speed that outstripped Mr Clarence's Cadillac, following behind.

Portimao looked interesting under the bright sunshine; Eugenia looking out of the small window, hoping she might have time to explore it, but that seemed unlikely.

The hospital was small, tucked away in the centre of the town, but the room they were led to was bright and airy, and Eugenia lost no time in making her patient comfortable. Dr da Marcos came with Mr Grenfell presently, accompanied by another older man, who was introduced as the anaesthetist. They stood around talking pleasantly, taking it in turns to examine Mrs Clarence, making cheerful remarks as they did so. 'There's no reason why you shouldn't be in England for Easter,' observed Mr Grenfell. 'You have two boys at school, I believe?'

Mrs Clarence's pale face lighted. 'Oh, do you really think so? I should love that—and to feel well again.'

He smiled gently. 'I can see no obstacle. It will be up to you, once the operation is over, to get fit as quickly as possible. In three weeks' time you should be fit to travel.'

He got up from the side of the bed. 'We'll leave you to Sister, now. Presently she'll go away for a little while to have her lunch, but in the meantime Dr da Marcos will bring you your other nurse, Amalia Deniz, so that you can get to know each other. She speaks English.'

He went away, and presently Dr da Marcos came back with a pretty dark girl with a smiling face, who shook hands with Eugenia and then with her patient. The three of them talked for a few minutes and then Eugenia took her on one side. 'Shall I explain Mr Grenfell's methods now?' she asked. 'And may I call you Amalia, and you call me Eugenia if you will,' and when the other girl agreed readily: 'Good, now here are the charts—I'm to stay with Mrs Clarence until midnight, but I'm only next door, so don't mind calling me if you're worried or need help—it's so much easier with two. I'll give you a hand with the bed and so on in the morning before you go off at eight o'clock. Now this is what Mr Grenfell intends to do . . .'

Amalia was quick; she grasped the main points at once. 'I have never seen this operation,' she observed. 'They always go to Lisbon.'

'Yes, I know, but Mrs Clarence is too ill to stand such a long journey. You'll go back with her to her home, won't you? I shall be there for a day or two, but we have to go back to England in a week's time.'

Someone came to take her to lunch presently, an early meal so that she would have time to get Mrs Clarence ready for theatre. She wasn't very hungry and she sat alone in a small dining room filled with tables, presumably where the hospital staff had their meals. She ate the fish and rather sweet custard tart and drank some black coffee, then went back to Mrs Clarence, fretful now and a little frightened. Luckily it was time to give the pre-med. Eugenia and Amalia put on gowns, tied back their hair, talking gently the while, and then put on Mrs Clarence's gown and slid the needle expertly into the thin arm.

An hour later Eugenia was in theatre, gowned and masked and scrubbed up and decidedly peevish. Mr Grenfell had omitted to tell her that she was expected to scrub for the operation. She had supposed that there would be a theatre nurse to do that, and indeed the nurse in charge had scrubbed as well, explaining cheerfully to Eugenia that she had never seen open chest surgery—all such cases went to Lisbon, and although she was eager to assist she was glad Eugenia was taking the case. Eugenia didn't share the gladness; she hadn't scrubbed for quite some time. It would serve Mr Grenfell right if she made a mess of it.

She didn't, of course. They worked together, speaking rarely, relaxed and at ease with each other. Mr Grenfell worked without haste and finally stood back to allow his assistant to finish the stitching. 'She'll do,' he said, and then: 'Thank you, Sister.' He began to pull off his gloves. 'I'll see you in the room they've set up for intensive care. Go with the patient.'

He sounded coldly polite, and Eugenia, peeling off her own gloves wondered why she should feel unhappy about that.

CHAPTER THREE

EUGENIA was kept busy for some time. There were the tubes to keep a sharp eye on, the blood transfusion to regulate and continuous oxygen to control. Amalia had been waiting for them and Eugenia had been glad of her skilled help. The anaesthetist and Mr Grenfell came in together within minutes of them getting Mrs Clarence positioned in her bed, examined her briefly, pronounced themselves satisfied and went away again. It was just a question of waiting for her to come round from the anaesthetic before propping her up on her pillows.

'It's all over, Mrs Clarence,' Eugenia told her as she opened her eyes and stared up at her in a woolly fashion. 'Everything is fine; just lie still and go to sleep again. I'll be here . . .'

Mrs Clarence grunted and closed her eyes again, and a few minutes later Mr Grenfell came back. 'Mrs Clarence regained consciousness two minutes ago,' Eugenia told him, and added blood pressure, pulse and respirations.

He nodded. 'Good.' He looked across at Amalia, on the other side of the bed. 'Will you take over for ten minutes while Sister Smith has a cup of tea?'

Amalia nodded earnestly. 'I have the bell,' she stated. 'Eugenia will come.'

There was a small ante-room outside the ward; someone had set a tray there with tea and a plate of cakes, and Mr Grenfell pulled a chair across and told her to sit down. There were two cups on the tray and when she glanced at him enquiringly, he said, 'Yes, please, pour me a cup too, will you?' He sat down opposite her. 'You did very well in theatre, Eugenia.'

He had never called her Eugenia before, but she let that pass. 'I would have done even better if I'd known that I was to scrub,' she pointed out.

He waved that aside. 'Rubbish!' He ate one of the cakes from the plate she had offered. 'I'll stay here for the night—you'll be on duty until midnight and be ready to give a hand if you're wanted. Don't let anyone else touch the tubes except yourself, they'll be in for forty-eight hours; if the bottles need changing, do it yourself. If there's more than three hundred mls. in six hours' time, I'm to be told at once—you know all this, inside out and back to front, but I'm making sure. This isn't quite like our home ground, so no offence meant.'

She smiled at him. 'No offence taken,' she told him cheerfully. 'I'm glad the operation was a success.'

'Early days, to be sure, but we caught it in time.' He drank the rest of his tea and got to his feet as she put down her cup. 'We'll have another look, shall we?'

Amalia went off duty soon after that. It had been arranged that a nurse would come if Eugenia rang the bell. 'And I'll be in and out during the night,' said Mr Grenfell, disappearing through the door.

He came twice before midnight and again as she was making a careful check with Amalia. Everything was going well. Mrs Clarence, well sedated, was sleeping and the paraphernalia surrounding her was functioning just as it should. 'Go to bed,' said Mr Grenfell, and Eugenia, with a muttered 'Goodnight', went.

The next forty-eight hours were vital to Mrs Clarence's recovery, and Eugenia, beyond a brief sleep and meals eaten as quickly as possible, had no leisure. But at the end of that time, with her patient free from tubes, bottles and oxygen mask, sitting up groggily in a chair, she was able to relax.

Mr Grenfell, coming, the epitome of the well dressed gentleman, at half past seven in the morning on the third day, pronounced himself satisfied and well pleased with his patient. The look he cast at Eugenia wasn't so satisfied, however. He said abruptly: 'You've had no off duty, have you, Eugenia? I think tomorrow you must have a free day. Everything is going well, another twelve hours and we can start thinking about getting Mrs Clarence back home. I'm entirely confident of Dr da Marcos's handling of the case, and Amalia is admirably suited to taking over from you. After today you and I will take back seats.'

He didn't stop to hear if she had anything to say but disappeared through the door.

It would be nice to have a day to herself, thought Eugenia tiredly. She had gulped in the fresh spring air for five minutes after her meal breaks and had longed to get out of uniform and go a long walk—somewhere along the coast, in the rather wild country leading down to the shore. Of course that would be too far, but she would certainly explore the town and walk along the boulevard towards the sea. Praia da Rocha was only a mile or so away, Amalia had told her, with its lovely beach and little shops. Too cold to swim, of course, she had added, but Eugenia, looking at the bright sunshine outside, thought it would be warm enough to walk along the sands and have coffee outside a café. Which reminded her that she had no money—Mr Grenfell had said he would see to all that, but he hadn't mentioned it again. She would have to find time to ask him before the morning.

He came again at midday with Dr da Marcos and there was no chance to speak to him, only to answer his abrupt questions and listen to his instructions, but that evening he came alone and sat down beside Mrs Clarence with the air of a man who had time on his hands.

'Another two or three days and you'll be feeling well enough to go home,' he promised her. 'Sister Smith and I will stay until then and after that Dr da Marcos and Amalia will take over. You've done very well—go carefully, and don't do more than Dr da Marcos allows—when you come to England at Easter I'll give you a check-up.'

Mrs Clarence beamed at him from a still wan face. 'I'll never be able to thank you both enough for all you've done, nor will my husband. That first day when Eugenia got me into a chair and I could have screamed at her—because all I wanted to do was to lie still and die, but now I know that she was keeping me alive. You have no idea what it feels like to be given a second chance . . .'

'Yes, I do,' said Mr Grenfell seriously, and she said contritely: 'Oh, of course you do—it's you who gives people like me that chance . . .'

'I wouldn't be able to do it without Eugenia or Amalia or Dr da Marcos.'

Mrs Clarence turned to look at Eugenia, standing quietly by. 'Such a beautiful girl too—quite wasted on miseries like me!'

'Mrs Clarence, I can assure you that Eugenia will not be wasted.' He got up and strolled to the door, ignoring Eugenia's enquiring look. It was a minute or two before she remembered that she hadn't asked for some money; she said breathlessly to Mrs Clarence: 'I won't be two ticks,' and flew out of the door after him. He was at the end of the passage talking to the anaesthetist, but he looked round enquiringly as she reached them.

'Forgotten something, Sister?' he asked.

'Tomorrow—if I'm to have a free day—I haven't any Portuguese money. You did say . . .'

'I'll see you in the morning.' He spoke pleasantly, but she felt herself dismissed. With her head seething with plans to leave the hospital without waiting for his convenience—she could surely get her English money changed—she went back to her patient.

'You do look cross,' commented Mrs Clarence.

Eugenia summoned up the sunniest of smiles. 'Oh, but I'm not—I'll get your morning drink and have mine with you. Mr Clarence will be here soon, won't he? I'll do your face first, if you like, a little blusher on your cheeks and that new wrap he brought you. You look pretty good to me. I'll wash your hair this evening if you feel like it . . .'

The day went well. It was nice to see Mrs Clarence improving almost by the hour—she had a long way to go, of course, but she was well on the way to convalescence now, another two or three days and Eugenia supposed she and Mr Grenfell would go back to England. But first, she thought with delight, she had a whole day in which to explore even this tiny corner of Portugal. She had no plans; a quick look at Portimao as soon as she had had breakfast, and then a bus to the beach and a walk on the shore. She handed over to Amalia, had her supper and went to her austere little room, her head full of plans, but too tired to bother with them.

She took a look at Mrs Clarence when she got up in the morning. The night, Amalia reported, had gone well, and the charts showed the gradual, undramatic improvement they all hoped for. The day nurse would be on presently, a quiet serious girl Eugenia had already met and instructed about Mr Grenfell's methods. She went back and dressed, had a sketchy breakfast, collected her handbag and sunglasses and left the hospital, walking into a bright sunny morning, already pleasantly warm.

The hospital was in the centre of the town, its courtyard surrounded by high walls, pierced by tall wrought iron gates, left open. Eugenia stood for a moment on the pavement, wondering whether to go left or right, when a ramshackle Simca drew up beside her.

'There you are,' said Mr Grenfell; his tone implied that she had kept him waiting. 'Get in, then, if we're to make the most of our day.'

Eugenia made no attempt to move. 'Get in?' she queried. 'Why? I'm going to explore the town and then go to the beach at Praia da Rocha.'

'What an ungrateful girl you are! I've taken the trouble to get a car for the day—I thought we'd drive along the coast to Cape St Vincent, an absolute must for the tourist, and then take a look at Henry the Navigator's place—it's close by. Then there's Sagres. We can lunch there before driving up through the mountains to Monchique—a very restful and rural place. But of course, if you had your heart set on peering into shop windows, I'll have to go by myself.'

He contrived to look so forlorn that her kind heart was touched. She said carefully: 'It sounds delightful, if you're sure you'd like me to come . . . It'll be all day,' she added doubtfully.

'All day,' he agreed gravely, 'but I daresay we'll be able to rub along if we try hard enough.' He held the door open more widely. 'Get in.'

She did so, telling herself it would be silly to refuse such a chance to see so much of the surrounding country; she might get the opportunity of a visit to the town before they left.

'Read anything about this part of the world?' asked
Mr Grenfell.

'I've hardly had the time . . .'

'Well, the fashionable end of the coast is behind us—
there are several popular beaches and small seaside
towns between here and St Vincent, but most people go
to Faro or Albufeira. There's a large luxury hotel at
Praia da Rocha, but further along the coast it isn't as
grand, and much nicer.'

He was urging the little car along the road towards
the sea, past the old fortress of St Catherine and then
along the boulevard by the beach. There were a few
people there, for it was warm enough to sit in the sun
even at that early hour, but it was a glorious beach, and
the wide sweep of the sea took Eugenia's attention as
they drove round the bay to Lagos.

There was another river here; she craned her neck to
see it as they swept over a bridge and entered the town.
'Coffee,' said Mr Grenfell, and parked the car on a
corner of waste ground. 'Through here,' he told her,
and took her arm to lead her through a narrow lane
which opened into a cobbled square, lined with shops
and shaded by orange trees.

Eugenia stood and gaped, oranges and orange
blossom on the same trees was something to gape at,
but she wasn't given time to look around her for more
than a few minutes. He sat her down at one of the little
tables outside a café and ordered coffee from a hovering
waiter.

'Have you any idea where we're going?' He frowned.
'You said you'd had no chance . . .'

'Not since we came,' she told him calmly. 'Before we
left I looked at a map. I do know that we're going
due west and then turn north into the mountains, but
I know nothing about the towns or the people or

food . . .' She sipped her coffee, dark and strong in a little cup. 'You've been here before, I expect?'

'Yes, I don't know much about the eastern end of the coast, but I've stayed around here several times.' He added a little impatiently: 'Do you want to stop for half an hour and look at the shops?'

'No, thank you.' She sounded convincingly certain, although she glanced with regret at a nearby shop window, filled with delicate embroidery. There was bound to be a shop very similar in Portimao.

They went back to the car and he took the road west, through groves of almonds and fig trees, past narrow lanes leading down to the sea and the small villages there. There were a few villas here and a lack of any land development, only a rather wild country which Eugenia loved. When they reached Vila do Bispo, Mr Grenfell observed: 'This is the last village of any size before Cape St Vincent—we'll go there first, and then we'll go to Sagres and look at Prince Henry's Fort.'

Cape St Vincent looked forbidding and bleak; there was a lighthouse at its tip and several stalls selling knitted jackets and caps and embroidery. Eugenia was swept past them, given a swift tour of the lighthouse, and urged back into the car. The short drive around the bay to the other side to Cape Sagres was wholly occupied in asking qustions, answered goodnaturedly enough by Mr Grenfell.

Prince Henry's Fort was far too interesting to hurry over; she lingered there, asking more questions, trying to imagine what it must have been like in the fifteenth century, sending ships to Madeira, the Azores, the west coast of Africa. She listened carefully to all that her companion had to say and when at length they left the place, she said: 'I must get a book about this and read it when I get back.'

'Or come back and see it for a second time,' he suggested casually.

'That would be nice.' Her voice was unknowingly wistful.

They had lunch at the *pousada* overlooking the beach at Sagres. It was a low white building with a red-tiled roof, charmingly furnished and, at that time of year, half empty. They ate octopus cooked in tomato sauce, although Mr Grenfell didn't tell Eugenia that until she had eaten every scrap of it and voted it delicious, and little tarts filled with thick custard and figs, and they drank a local wine, pale and rather too dry for her taste. The coffee was dark and thick. 'Not at all like Nescafé,' remarked Mr Grenfell, 'but when in Rome . . .' He smiled at her and it struck her that he was really rather a pleasant companion. 'There's a small *estalagem* in the Monchique mountains where one can get a splendid pot of tea. We'll go there on our way back.'

They didn't linger over their meal; it was early afternoon by now and pleasantly warm, but as they climbed towards Silves, it grew cooler, but the country was delightful with its trees and small houses tucked away by the side of the road. Mr Grenfell stopped at the summit of a hill overlooking the town. 'Moorish,' he observed, 'liberated in the thirteenth century. That enormous building in the centre is their old fort and the cathedral is next to it.' He started the car again and went slowly down the hill and then into the town of white-walled houses and presently parked close to the cathedral.

'Not bored?' he asked as they crossed the road and went inside.

Eugenia shook her head. 'It's all marvellous; if only I can remember this day!'

He stopped halfway down the aisle of the great building, 'I shall remember it,' he told her quietly.

They spent some time there, not talking much, and then looked round the fort before going back to the car. As they got in Eugenia observed: 'I thought it would be cooler—we're going up into the hills, aren't we?'

'Yes, but Silves is in a hollow, it can be very hot here in the summer; it will get cooler again as we climb.'

The road wound through cork trees, orange groves and eucalyptus trees going gently uphill, and presently they passed the small spa of Caldas, used in Roman times, revived during the eighteenth century and once again falling into gentle decay, although they saw there was a small modern hospital there where patients went for the treatment of rheumatism and to take the waters.

Nevertheless they didn't stop there, but followed the ever-climbing road until they reached Monchique. Eugenia was enchanted by the sight of it, little houses built in terraces, the spring flowers and shrubs, the magnificent view towards the coast behind them and so far below. They wandered round the small square and she bought postcards and obediently drank Madronho, distilled from arbutus berries. She didn't like it over-much, but Mr Grenfell seemed to expect her to drink it.

'It's so far from everywhere,' she said, unable to put into words what she meant. 'It's a different world ...'

Mr Grenfell agreed gravely, lent his pen so that she could write her cards and suggested that they might climb another mile or so and have tea at the *estalagem* Abrigo da Montanha.

The road wound uphill, giving a magnificent view of the coast in the distance, and presently he parked the car and trod up a narrow path to the *estalagem*, and since it was still warm in the afternoon sun, they had tea on its terrace.

'What a heavenly spot,' declared Eugenia, 'just to stay here and roam around and come to this every evening.'

'You have simple tastes, Eugenia,' observed Mr Grenfell. 'No dancing or cabaret or disco?'

'No,' she shook her head. 'No—though I like dancing, but who would want to dance when there's all this to explore?' She waved an arm at the surrounding countryside. 'I won't forget it.'

Mr Grenfell's eyes gleamed beneath their lids. 'And nor shall I.'

They went back presently, travelling the eighteen miles or so to Portimao without haste, stopping here and there to scan the country below them, stopping again at a wayside shop, where Eugenia bought a little knitted wrap and a hand-carved box for her father. 'I'll get sweets for the twins in Portimao,' she explained to Mr Grenfell. 'They like chewing things.' She added unguardedly: 'Perhaps your fiancée would like a wrap— they're so pretty . . .'

She was instantly put in her place. 'Not quite Miriam's style,' said Mr Grenfell austerely.

They parted at the hospital entrance and Mr Grenfell received her thanks with a coolness that damped her pleasure in the day's outing, still further damped when she heard from Amalia, whom she met as she went in, that he had a dinner engagement and was already late for it. She thought guiltily of the time she had taken to choose the wrap; a garment which he so obviously despised as not worthy of his Miriam.

Mrs Clarence, once she got going, made great strides; two days later she was put into an ambulance and driven carefully back to her home with Eugenia in close attendance. Amalia was to take over in a couple of days' time, when she had had a free day or two, and Mr Grenfell and Eugenia would return to England. The whole thing had been highly successful; Mr Clarence could find no words to express his gratitude and Mrs Clarence, still weak, was already planning her trip to England to see the boys during the Easter holidays.

Eugenia had seen very little of Mr Grenfell; he came and went frequently enough, but the talk was solely of their patient and he addressed her austerely as Sister Smith. It was hard to remember that he was the same pleasant companion who had spent the day with her. When he appeared soon after breakfast the day after Mrs Clarence was back home and informed her that they would be leaving in two days' time, she said merely: 'Very well, sir, I'll have another session with Amalia and make quite sure she understands, although she's a splendid nurse . . .'

'Do that. Do it in the morning; you mustn't leave Portugal without seeing the sea caves at Ponte de Piedade—we'll go there after lunch.'

'I have to pack,' said Eugenia matter-of-factly.

He opened his eyes. 'One case? Surely a matter of minutes?'

It sounded tempting. Perhaps he was bored with his own company. 'That would be nice,' said Eugenia primly.

It was another glorious day: early April now and pleasantly warm. It was only a short distance to Lagos, but they didn't stop there, but went through the town, towards Ponte de Piedade, where Mr Grenfell stopped the car, urged her to get out and got out himself. 'We'll walk,' he observed, and glanced down at her feet. She was thankful that she had had the sense to wear low-heeled sensible shoes.

It meant a good deal of scrambling and climbing

down towards the sea, but the caves were worth it, and Eugenia, quite carried away, took off her shoes and tights and paddled in the chilly water when they reached the beach.

'I could stay here for ever!' she exclaimed happily, and turned a beaming face to his. 'Isn't it heaven?'

There was a look on his face which she had never seen before; he said softly: 'Yes, and I've only just discovered it.'

'Oh, haven't you been here before? Do we have to climb through those rocks to get back to where you left the car?'

She skipped on ahead of him, whistling under her breath, happier than she had been for a long time. No thought of Humphrey entered her head, certainly no thought of getting married, and St Clare's never entered her head either—full as it was of fabulous daydreams. They were half way back from the shore when she stopped suddenly. Someone had moaned, and as she listened, moaned again.

Mr Grenfell had heard it too; he came and stood beside her, motioned her to silence and stood listening. The moan came again, and he walked away from her and knelt down on the rough grass. Eugenia came carefully after him and got down beside him—and saw the half-hidden hole.

'Of course,' said Mr Grenfell, 'the caves run back a good distance. Now I wonder . . .'

'I'll go down,' said Eugenia at once. 'You'll never get through that hole.'

Mr Grenfell laughed. 'Watch me,' he commanded, and slid over its edge and out of sight.

'Mr Grenfell—oh, Mr Grenfell, where have you gone?' She could hear the panic in her voice but was powerless to stop it.

'Don't be a goose!' Mr Grenfell's voice, faintly mocking, floated reassuringly upwards. 'You'll have to come down too, Eugenia. There's a lad here—broken leg, I imagine, and concussed. Come down feet first, I'll catch you.'

She really had no choice; she lowered herself cautiously and felt his hands guiding her down and then lifting her. It was dim in the cave, she couldn't see into the farthest corners, but she could hear rustlings which she didn't like, but since Mr Grenfell seemed to think she was made of the same stern stuff as he was, she said nothing, but turned her attention to the boy on the ground. He must have fallen through the hole above them, because his leg was bent at an unnatural angle and there was a lump on his temple and a deep cut, still oozing blood.

'The leg first,' said Mr Grenfell. 'We have no splint, so we shall have to tie his legs together. Let me have your belt.'

Eugenia unbuckled the soft leather belt she had saved to buy herself; it had cost more than she could afford and she had justified its purchase by the knowledge that it would last her for a number of years. Apparently not; she handed it over to Mr Grenfell, who took it with as little interest as though it had been a nice piece of string, and began, very carefully, to straighten out the boy's leg. 'Very nasty,' he commented, as he took a penknife from his pocket and cut the belt in two. 'Take a pull on the foot, Eugenia, we'll have to get it as straight as possible before we haul him up.'

It took some time, but the boy was still unconscious. 'A fortunate thing,' Mr Grenfell declared, 'and let's hope he stays that way until we've got him out of here.'

Eugenia tied Mr Grenfell's clean handkerchief round the boy's cut head. 'How?' she asked.

'Well, I'll have to go first—I'll lean him up against the rock and you'll have to lift his arms as high as you can so that I can get a grip on them. It won't do his leg any good, but there's no other way.'

Eugenia, aware of the faint rustling in the darker recesses of the cave, said suddenly in a squeaky voice. 'I think there are rats here . . .'

'Well, of course there are,' Mr Grenfell sounded impatient, 'what do you expect in a cave?'

'I'm very afraid of rats,' said Eugenia, her voice a little high.

'Bunkum, a great girl like you!'

No comfort at all—indeed, an insult. She seethed silently.

Mr Grenfell began to heave the boy against the wall of the cave. 'Don't think about them,' he advised her kindly, and began to claw his way upward. 'Don't let him slide back,' he advised, and went on his difficult way, dislodging clods of earth and stones as he went. Just for a moment she thought he would slide back again, but he was a powerful man, she let out a held breath as he hauled himself over the rim of the hole. A moment later his head appeared over its edge.

'Lift his arms,' he commanded 'as high as you can, and when I say so, give him a good shove upwards from behind.' A rat squeaking from behind gave her added strength, and then there was no sound save that of Mr Grenfell's heavy breathing as he hauled slowly on the boy. It seemed an age before the unconscious youth disappeared slowly from view and endless seconds before Mr Grenfell's head appeared once more.

'Up you come!' He leaned over dangerously and stretched out his great arms. 'Catch hold.'

She forgot the rats for the moment. 'I weigh a ton,' she told him.

'An exaggeration. A hefty girl, perhaps, but where would I have been with a willowy damsel with no more strength than a kitten?'

She scrambled around for a footing and slipped back. 'Mr Grenfell, I can't . . .'

His voice, very calm, floated down to her. 'Does it not strike you that "Mr Grenfell" is perhaps a little formal in circumstances such as these? My name is Gerard. Now stop flapping around, there's a good girl, dig in your toes and come on up here—we've got to get this boy to hospital.'

Eugenia tried again, and this time Mr Grenfell caught her by the wrists. 'Heave ho!' he said cheerfully, and suited the action to the words.

It was a slow business, although she helped as much as she could, clutching at bits of rock, the backs of her legs aching, but presently she landed in an untidy, sprawling heap on her face and content to stay that way; her arms felt as though they had been dragged from their sockets and she was covered in scratches and grazes.

'Up you get,' said Mr Grenfell, 'we've got work to do.'

'Stop bullying me,' puffed Eugenia, 'what do you take me for? Rats ready to gnaw me, and my new belt in ribbons, and now I haven't any skin on my knees or elbows . . .'

'Why do women exaggerate?' asked Mr Grenfell of no one in particular. 'And what about this poor lad?'

She got to her feet. 'I'm sorry, Mr Grenfell, what a wretched little beast I am. Shall I take his legs?'

'If I carry him, could you walk beside me and support his legs? Hold them as straight as you possibly can—we've not got far to go to the car, and we can wedge him on the back seat and have him in hospital in no time at all.'

He stooped to lift the boy and waited while she got a firm hold of his legs. 'And no more Mr Grenfell, I beg. Let's leave that for the wards.'

Their progress was slow and by the time they had reached the car Eugenia was exhausted. Not that she was allowed to give way to that.

'In the back,' said Mr Grenfell, and he slid the boy carefully along the seat, 'and you get into the front, Eugenia.' Without appearing to do so he gave her a sidelong glance; she was pale from her exertions and her hands were scratched and filthy dirty. Her tidy head was no longer tidy and her face badly needed a wash. All the same, she still looked beautiful.

'Perhaps not quite the afternoon's outing we expected, but an interesting one nevertheless,' observed Mr Grenfell, starting the car.

'Interesting? I wouldn't call it that,' said Eugenia. 'Exciting and sad for the boy, and heavenly paddling in the sea—I won't forget it. Now how will they find out who the boy is?'

'I imagine someone will tell the police—he'll be in good hands.'

She glanced over her shoulder at the still form. 'Poor lad—I'm glad we found him.'

'Yes—it was a chance in a hundred, wasn't it? Not many people go that way at this time of year, and of course he wasn't in a condition to shout.' He glanced at her. 'Will you be sorry to go, Eugenia?'

'Oh, yes, I've loved it—the people have been so kind, and it's so satisfying to know that Mrs Clarence will be all right—even more satisfying for you. St Clare's is going to be a bit drear . . .'

'You'll have Humphrey,' said Mr Grenfell soothingly.

Her, 'Yes', was a bit doubtful.

'He may even decide to marry you out of hand,' suggested Mr Grenfell.

'Why ever should he do that?'

'To make sure of you.' He turned the car into the hospital yard. 'Here we are. Go along to Casualty and warn someone, will you? I'll carry him in.'

The house doctor on duty took charge, the police were warned and Eugenia, feeling she was no longer needed, slipped away towards the private wing where she had her room. It was early evening by now and she was hungry; supper was only half an hour away and she would have to clean herself up. It would have been nice, she thought, standing under the shower, if Mr Grenfell—no, Gerard—had invited her to have a meal with him somewhere. Perhaps if they hadn't discovered the boy, he would have done so. She cleaned up her scratched hands, put plasters on her knees and elbows and got into a skirt and thin sweater. She wouldn't have accepted anyway, she told herself, she still had to pack her case and do her nails and wash her hair, and tomorrow was a full day's duty . . .

She was going out of the dining room, an hour later, when she met Mr Grenfell. He stopped squarely in front of her, so that she couldn't get by unless she pushed past him.

'I considered taking you out to supper, but decided against it,' he told her. 'I think that in the circumstances, it would have been a stupid thing to do.'

Eugenia felt outraged feelings swelling to bursting point inside her. 'Not nearly as stupid as I'd have been if I'd accepted!' she snapped, and since she couldn't get past him, she turned on her heel and swept back into the dining room. Which meant that it took her quite a time to find her way through the kitchen and out the other side into the private wing again.

Bed seemed the only place to be. She undressed and bounced into bed, still fuming; a good thing the case was finished and she could go back to Humphrey. Only somehow Humphrey wasn't very clear in her mind, ousted in fact by Mr Grenfell's handsome, remote features. The moment she got back, she promised herself, she would persuade Humphrey to marry her; never mind the tumble-dryer and the fitted carpets, they could come later. To get married and away from Mr Grenfell was suddenly very important.

CHAPTER FOUR

EUGENIA wasn't to get away from Mr Grenfell as quickly as all that. There he was when she went on duty in the morning, sitting on her patient's bed, absorbed in a lighthearted discussion which was making Mrs Clarence chuckle a good deal. When she saw Eugenia she called: 'Good morning, dear. Come and convince this man that there are still a number of women left in the world who would rather get married and look after a husband and children than hold down some highly paid job, or worse, swan around doing nothing.'

Eugenia said lightly: 'Well, I wouldn't mind swanning around, looking like one of the top-ranking models—not for keeps, though; just to see what it felt like.'

Mr Grenfell turned and raked her with a deliberate glance. 'Most of the models I've met are extremely thin, one might say almost skinny—you'd hardly qualify, Eugenia.'

Mrs Clarence laughed at what she thought was a nice little joke; Eugenia might be a big girl, but she had a lovely figure, and she didn't believe for one minute that Mr Grenfell was unaware of that. Eugenia laughed too and gave him a look to slay him; it was certainly important that she got hold of Humphrey the moment she got back ... 'I'll see about your breakfast,' she said with well held calm. 'That is, if Mr Grenfell is going?'

He had gone by the time she got back, and the morning was taken up with getting Mrs Clarence up, making her bed and encouraging her to walk on the balcony outside her room, and after lunch, once she was tucked up for her nap, there was Amalia to make her final suggestions to and the charts to bring up to date. There would be no time in the morning, they were to leave directly after breakfast, Mr Grenfell, meeting her briefly during the evening, told her, adding that he had a dinner date and must on no account miss it. 'I daresay Humphrey will manage to be free and take you out,' he said blandly.

Eugenia agreed pleasantly, although she didn't feel very pleasant. Mr Grenfell's remarks about her size still rankled, and over and above that, she was only too well aware that it was very unlikely that Humphrey would do anything of the sort. She had only been away for little over a week; no cause for celebrations.

Her misgivings were more than justified. Back at St Clare's, her case unpacked, her uniform tidily ready for the morning, she lay in bed and thought about her day. They had left the hospital directly after breakfast, on her part with some regret, for she had been very happy there and she would have liked to have seen Mrs Clarence quite recovered before wishing her goodbye. Mr Grenfell had been at his most impersonal, attending to her comfort with grave courtesy, smoothing their journey apparently without effort, and never once making a remark to which she could have taken exception. The Bentley had been waiting for them when they arrived at Heathrow and she had had nothing to do but be guided through Customs and out to where it was parked. And once in the car, she had been unable to think of anything to say. It wasn't until they were actually outside the hospital entrance that she managed: 'That was a very pleasant journey, Mr Grenfell, thank you.' After a brief pause she added: 'You're in good time for your appointment.'

He turned to look at her as he brought the car to a halt. 'And you? Time enough to phone your Humphrey and have a quiet dinner together, I hope.' He got out and opened her door. 'I'll see that your case is sent up to your room. I shall see you on the ward in the morning.' And at her rather startled look: 'It will be round day, or had you forgotten?'

'No—yes, that is, I hadn't thought about it,' said Eugenia. 'I'd better go to the office.'

He nodded and went round to the boot. It was obvious that he had nothing more to say to her; she had pushed open the doors and crossed the entrance hall and made her way, feeling vaguely put out, to the nurses' home.

Humphrey had been off duty and she had arranged to meet him after supper—a noisy meal, since her friends clamoured to hear her news. She had left them feeling cheerful, anxious to tell Humphrey all about it too, but one look at his face damped her good spirits at once.

Humphrey was coldly furious. 'You told me a week,' he said at once, turning a cold cheek to her kiss. 'It's nine days—I suppose you've been taking a few days off and enjoying yourself?'

She said gently: 'No, darling, I've been working until the last moment. Mrs Clarence—the patient, you know—is only just out of the wood; I should have liked to have stayed longer, but Mr Grenfell had an appointment for this evening.' And probably even now he's dallying with the glamorous Miriam, she thought silently; not that he didn't deserve a little light relief after his hard work.

'Mother found it very strange, to say the least,' declared Humphrey sulkily. 'You had no business to go gallivanting off in that fashion . . .'

'I didn't gallivant,' protested Eugenia tiredly. 'I worked hard with no time off.'

'Just as I thought!' burst out Humphrey. 'Making use of you, taking advantage of your good nature!'

'Oh, it wasn't like that at all,' she said. 'On one of the last days I was free all day.' She realised her mistake as she said it, for Humphrey demanded at once:

'What did you do?'

'Well, Mr Grenfell hired a car and we drove along the Algarve coast. It was delightful; beautiful scenery and much warmer than it is here.'

Humphrey snorted. 'I'm hurt and vexed,' he told her pompously. 'I hope this sort of thing won't occur again.'

'But I've done nothing wrong,' Eugenia cried, 'and you're making such a fuss about nothing—you haven't even said you're glad to see me again.' She had been suddenly furious. 'I'm going to bed.' And she had flounced off, back into the hospital and up to her room, to cry her eyes out, although she hadn't been quite sure why she had cried, and by now she was too tired to wonder about that, so with a final sniff she closed her eyes and slept.

There was no time to worry about Humphrey, or anything else for that matter, once she was on the ward. Hatty was waiting for her, full of important information she must assimilate before Mr Grenfell arrived. They went over the charts together before Eugenia did her round, greeting patients who were still there and getting to know her new ones. She had them all nicely sorted out by the time the clock struck and she started down the ward, to be met by Mr Grenfell, as impassive as always. Beneath her usual calm manner she found herself feeling strangely disturbed; it was ridiculous that the sight of him, his large figure so elegant, his expression so impersonally kind, even his habit of jingling the small change in his pocket while he listened quietly to whatever was being said to him, should be the reason for it. After all, she had seen him looking exactly as he did now for three years, week in, week out, and had been quite unmoved.

Perhaps it was because he seemed a different man from the one who had hauled her out of that awful hole, crying 'Heave ho!' so cheerfully and actually calling her a hefty girl. Eugenia frowned fiercely at the memory of it, and became all at once aware of the silence around her. They were all looking at her; the routine of years, altered even by a few seconds, was enough to upset them. She said briskly: 'There are two new patients, sir, admitted during the night. Do you wish to see them first?'

The round went smoothly. Mr Grenfell took his time over the new patients, spent five minutes exchanging pleasantries with Mrs Dunn, now happily free from her tubes and intent on getting home. And with Barbara ready for discharge to a convalescent home, and quite animated now, they stood around her chair and joked gently before he left the ward and went into the office.

There was the usual amount of writing to do, notes to make, charts to study. It was all of half an hour before he and Harry and one of his housemen got up to go. Mr Grenfell, the last through the door, paused, came back into the little room, carefully closing the door behind him, and asked her: 'Well, did you enjoy your evening out with Humphrey?'

Eugenia had remained standing when the rest of them had got up to go. Now she turned her back on him and looked out of the window, presumably to admire the rows of chimneypots which comprised all the view there was.

'We didn't have an evening out,' she told him in a wooden voice.

'Humphrey on call? Hard luck.' He sounded so cheerful that she could have thrown something at him.

'No, he was free,' she said deliberately. 'He—we had a difference of opinion . . .'

'Oh, Mother. Am I right?'

'Well, partly.' She turned round to look at him. 'Humphrey didn't want me to go in the first place—I told you that.'

'I hadn't forgotten. But surely, since you came back safely, virtue intact and your pretty head unturned by the soft living and the easy life, he felt like celebrating?'

She blushed faintly. 'Well, he didn't. But I expect he'll feel better about it by the time we see each other again.' She asked politely: 'And you, sir? Did you have a pleasant evening?'

'Not so much pleasant as interesting. By the way, I have something for you. Mrs Clarence asked me to let you have it once we were back in England.' He took an envelope from his pocket and handed it to her. 'Open it.'

She obeyed him, although if she had had time to think about it she would probably have refused on principle. The letter inside was brief, the cheque accompanying it of a size sufficient to make her open her lovely eyes very wide indeed. 'I can't possibly . . .' she began, to be interrupted by Mr Grenfell's firm:

'Yes, you can. The Clarences would be deeply hurt if you don't. See it from their point of view—you helped save her life, and they want to thank you for that.' He stretched out a hand and took the letter from her unresisting hand. 'Just as I thought—you're to spend it upon yourself. Quite right too. It's obvious to me that instead of spending money on clothes, you're saving it towards something dull like a washing machine or a fitted wardrobe, and since this cheque is over and above your salary, you're quite at liberty to fling it away on a pair of shoes or something similar.'

'A pair of shoes?' gasped Eugenia. 'Why, good heavens, I can buy a whole new outit and have something over!'

'Can you? Miriam mentioned the sum she had spent on the shoes she was wearing the other evening—a similar amount to this cheque, but I believe her to be extravagant.'

Eugenia forgot for the moment that he was a senior consultant. 'Do you really think that I could spend this on me? There's the Spring Ball . . .' Her eyes shone with anticipation and she saw him smile a little.

'An excellent chance to splash out. I shall expect to be dazzled, Eugenia.'

He had gone, closing the door softly behind him, before she could answer that. Just as well, perhaps.

She tucked the cheque and the letter away and went back to work; time enough to decide just what she would buy. She was going home that evening, spending the night there, and coming on duty at two o'clock in the afternoon, so that Hatty could have a well deserved long weekend. She would tell her father and the twins and give them each a present, but somehow she had no urge to tell Humphrey. He would do either one of two things; insist that she should return the cheque, or insist, just as firmly, that she should put every penny of it into the bank towards their future.

It was lovely to be home, sitting in the shabby, comfortable sitting room, listening to the news Bruce and Becky were intent on giving her; their O level papers, and exactly what they had written, and what did she think of their chances of passing? And her father, telling her amusing little stories about the children at his school, and presently she told them about the cheque. 'Should I put it in the bank?' she asked her father.

'Certainly not. It's a gift, over and above your salary, and Mrs Clarence most certainly would wish you to use it for your own pleasure. Buy some pretty clothes, Eugenia; you've had nothing for some months.'

'That's what Mr Grenfell said.'

Her father glanced at her. 'Then he's a sensible man. Fit yourself out, and spend every last penny of it.' He added firmly: 'And don't feel you have to tell Humphrey first—give him a nice surprise.'

Eugenia paid the cheque into the bank on her way back to St Clare's in the morning, her head full of what she would buy. She had a half day on the Tuesday after Hatty got back; a good day on which to shop. She made several lists over the weekend, whittling them down to her final choice, impatient for Tuesday.

'You look pleased with yourself,' observed Humphrey, pausing on his way to the Medical Wing as she came back from dinner on Monday. 'Won the pools or something?'

She felt instantly guilty, as the remark was so near the mark. Indeed, she might have told him about the cheque, only at that moment Mr Grenfell wandered out of a door towards them and commandeered Humphrey about some patient on the medical side he had been asked to see later that day.

She didn't see Humphrey again that day, and she didn't waste time looking for him on Tuesday; she handed over to a refreshed Hatty, and ignoring her dinner, flew to her room, changed rapidly and hurried to catch a bus to Regent Street. She had four precious hours in which to spend her cheque, and she had every intention of doing just that.

It wasn't difficult, of course. It was marvellous what money in your pocket did for you. She found the dress she wanted almost at once—a rich burgundy taffeta with a wide skirt and what was, for her, a daring neckline. Humphrey wasn't going to approve and his mother would probably faint with outraged modesty. It would make a nice change, thought Eugenia, prowling around the shoe department for matching satin sandals; nothing but straps and a three-inch heel and an outrageous price, but exactly what she wanted.

There was still money to spend. She found a jacket and skirt in an impractical pale blue and then searched for a knitting pattern and wool. She was an expert knitter and it would cost a quarter of the prices asked by the shops for the tempting sweaters and tops on display. She counted her change; enough for a pair of shoes if she didn't lose her head completely. She chose court shoes, plain and elegant and high-heeled—too high-heeled, she remembered as she stopped on the pavement and checked her list. She and Humphrey were exactly the same height; with heels like those, she would top him, even if only by an inch, and he wouldn't like that. All the same, she wasn't going to change them. Suddenly economically minded, she had decided to have tea in a small and rather seedy tea-shop and then she took herself back to St Clare's. It had been a lovely afternoon. She had spent almost every penny of the cheque and bought the kind of clothes which she had rejected for the last year or two because they were too fashionable and wouldn't last for more than a year.

She got off the bus, laden with her parcels, and walked across the hospital forecourt, slap into Mr Grenfell, who withstood her person with calm, studied her carefully and enquired unnecessarily, 'Been shopping?' He eyed her packages. 'No kitchen stove, no vacuum cleaner? Splendid! Probably I shan't recognise you at the Spring Ball—if I don't, be sure to give me a prod.'

He took most of the parcels from her and turned to walk back to the hospital entrance with her. 'I'm so glad you took my advice.'

'Yes, well, I asked my father and he agreed with you . . .'

'And Humphrey?' Mr Grenfell's voice was very bland.

Eugenia paused to look up at him. 'I haven't told him, and I feel terrible about it.'

'Well, don't. Just give him a delightful surprise at the Ball.' He handed the parcels over to a rather surprised porter who was passing. 'Take these over to the nurses' home for Sister Smith, will you? You can leave them in the warden's office there.'

Eugenia gaped at him. 'You can't do that!' she hissed urgently. 'Porters aren't allowed to do things for us . . .'

'Perhaps not, but I've yet to learn that they can't do things for me.' He then stood there, making no attempt to go, looking down at her. 'Are you free this evening?'

Eugenia felt sudden delight at the idea of going out with him, and then common sense took over. 'No—no, I'm afraid not—Humphrey's taking me out.'

His eyebrows rose a fraction and the corner of his mouth twitched. 'Then I must wish the pair of you a very pleasant evening, Eugenia.'

He turned away, and she started towards the corridor leading to the nurses' home, aware of regret and doing her best to stifle it. She hadn't gone a dozen steps before Mr Grenfell's large person confronted her once more.

'I can't resist the temptation to tell you you're a poor liar, Eugenia, and remind you that Humphrey is always on call on a Tuesday evening. I'm surprised that he—and you—have forgotten that. It would have been just as easy for you to have said you had no wish to spend the evening with me.'

She looked up at him, into his blandly smiling face, his eyes hooded, so that she had no idea what he was really thinking. And because she was an honest girl she blurted out: 'I should have liked to have gone out with you, Mr Grenfell—very much—only I don't think it's a very good idea. I couldn't think of any other excuse. I'm sorry.'

His smile widened. 'So am I. Ah, well, I suppose I'll have to make do with Miriam.'

Upon which outrageous remark he turned on his heel and walked away, this time through the door. Eugenia waited for a few moments, absurdly hoping that it would again open and that he would come back, but of course, he didn't.

Her heart should have leapt at the sight of Humphrey, obviously in a tearing hurry, white coat open, stethoscope stuffed in its pocket, a wodge of papers under one arm. That he had no time for her was obvious, only as he went past he gave her a look of utter surprise. She had smiled at him, but there was no answering glimmer on his face. Up to his eyes, poor dear, she thought, and felt guilty because she should have been overjoyed to see him, even for a moment, and all she had felt was a vague interest that he was there. Perhaps, she mused a little sadly, making her way up to her room, that was how one got when one had been engaged for too long with the prospect of marriage still in a future which seemed to become more and more remote.

It was the Spring Ball in four days' time, and there was a good deal of coming and going in the nurses' home. Evening finery was altered, ironed, added to, lengthened and shortened, and in some cases borrowed. Eugenia had kept quiet about her new dress. She had worn the only other one she had for so long that her friends had rather given up asking her what she would wear, and as for Humphrey, she saw him on the day following her shopping expedition, but he was far too busy telling her the ins and outs of a complicated case on one of the medical wards to do more than ask her why she had had so many parcels when they had met, and since he didn't wait for her to answer but began to explain just how he had counteracted the serious symptoms of his patient, she had remained silent.

All the more fun, she thought, dressing on the evening of the ball, because really the dress was quite something. She had had a busy day and it would have been nice to have had an hour or so leisure before getting ready. As it was, she had rushed off the ward as soon as she had given the night nurses the report, had a quick shower and got dressed. She didn't waste a great deal of time on her face and hair, she didn't use a great deal of make-up anyway, and she had washed her hair on the previous evening. She fastened the dress and studied herself in the wall mirror. Humphrey wasn't going to like that neck; the thought that Mr Grenfell was far more likely to appreciate it she instantly dismissed as frivolous. The sandals were lovely too; useless scraps of satin which filled her with the greatest pleasure. She switched out the light and went along to see if anyone else was ready.

The reception given to her appearance was more than gratifying. She was asked if she had robbed a bank, come up on the pools—even if she had broken off her engagement to Humphrey. 'He'll get a surprise, won't he?' demanded someone. 'I bet he'll marry you out of hand!'

Eugenia thought it unlikely. Humphrey never did anything on the spur of the moment or before he had carefully deliberated it; all the same, she was bursting to see his face when he saw her. They had arranged to meet just inside the door of the lecture hall where the dance was being held, and she saw him waiting as she went in. He had his back to her, but he turned as she walked towards him, his astonishment giving way to a frowning sternness which made her slow her steps. There was no one close by. He came very near to her and said in an angry voice: 'Eugenia, what on earth are you wearing? You aren't decent—and where did you get it?'

A small flame of anger made her beautiful eyes sparkle. 'Don't you like it? I bought it.' She lifted her skirts and showed him the ridiculous sandals. 'These too.'

'We agreed to spend as little as possible on clothes until we had all we want for a home of our own. These must have cost a small fortune, and you look ridiculous!'

She lifted her chin. She hadn't expected this; she had thought he might have been a little put out at first and then understood when she had explained to him, but Humphrey hadn't even asked her . . . 'Don't worry,' she told him tartly, 'I haven't used a farthing of my savings, and since you don't approve of me, then I'll find someone who does!'

She swept past him and joined a group of Sisters and housemen watching the dancing, and when a moment later, the younger of the surgical housemen asked her to dance, she did, turning her head away from Humphrey, standing like the wrath of God where she'd left him.

She was well liked by the younger housemen as well as the consulting staff, and she didn't lack for partners. It was an hour or more before she saw Mr Grenfell with his Miriam, and for once she felt equal to the occasion; her dress, while by no means haute couture, was a worthy match for Miriam's black satin sheath. She had, Eugenia considered, about as much shape as a runner bean and her shoulders were thin angles instead of being nicely rounded. She looked away quickly, though, not wanting Mr Grenfell to see her.

But he had. When the music started up again, he was there at her elbow, not even asking her if she wanted to dance, but whisking her off into the crowd on the floor.

He danced well. Eugenia, for all her size, was a good dancer too and followed him easily while she tried to think of something coolly firm about not having been asked. A waste of time, as it turned out, for Mr Grenfell said laconically: 'Don't bother, Eugenia; why bother with asking you to dance with me when I'm certain you'd like to?'

'Well,' she breathed, 'you really are the limit!'

He considered carefully. 'No. But I like my own way.'

They danced for a few minutes in silence. 'I haven't seen you dancing with Humphrey.' His voice was silky. 'Had a little lovers' tiff?'

'Don't be vulgar, Mr Grenfell!' and then, because she felt at ease with him and she wanted to unburden herself to someone: 'He doesn't like my dress, he says it's not decent—and that I shouldn't have bought it when we're saving for a home.'

'It is,' said Mr Grenfell in measured tones, 'a charming dress. I don't quite know what he considers decent—up to the chin and cut like a tent, perhaps? You have a glorious shape, Eugenia, and I can see no reason to hide it.' He glanced down at her. 'You seldom blush, but when you do, it's very fetching. I hope you spent the rest of the money on something as pretty as this dress.'

'Oh, I did, and I loved every minute of spending every penny. Father thought it was a good idea too.'

There was a decided gleam in Mr Grenfell's eyes. 'We older men can sometimes come up with good advice,' he told her. 'Have you had supper yet?'

'No. Harry said something about it . . .'

Mr Grenfell came to a beautifully controlled halt as the music stopped. 'Oh, he won't mind,' he observed, and took her by the arm. 'I'm hungry, aren't you?'

'Yes, but what about your fiancée?'

He waved a careless hand. 'Oh, the men are round her like flies round a honeypot.'

The dress had done something strange to Eugenia; Mr Grenfell had become Gerard and not the eminent surgeon she worked for. 'But don't you mind?' she demanded.

'Not particularly.'

She digested this in silence as they went down the corridor to the committee room where the food was. 'Well, no, perhaps not,' she said finally. 'I daresay you're very proud of her—I mean, because she attracts men . . .'

'I expect that's it,' he said blandly, and handed her a plate.

The tables were as yet only half filled; they sat down at a small one for two in the corner and ate their supper, talking about nothing much. They had almost finished when Harry came across the room.

He was on good terms with his chief and said, 'Hullo, sir,' in a manner both affable and polite, and then: 'Eugenia, I thought you were having supper with me.'

'I knew you wouldn't mind, Harry,' said Mr Grenfell cheerfully. 'Besides, the night is young. I daresay Eugenia will have worked up another appetite in an hour or two.' He added shamelessly: 'We had some things to discuss—a working supper, as it were.' He smiled widely: 'Draw up a chair and pile a plate—the food's very good.'

So the three of them sat there for another half hour until Harry suggested that Eugenia might like to dance again. 'Shake down that supper,' he observed. 'You don't want to burst the seams of that dress—I must say it's quite something. You're really quite a pretty girl.'

Eugenia's spirits had risen. Mr Grenfell might talk a lot of nonsense, but it had been soothing nonsense, and now here was Harry whom she had known for some years now and treated like a brother paying her compliments too. She went back to the hall and danced for the rest of the long evening, never lacking partners. Of Humphrey there was no sign, but what with the dress and the sandals and the traditional hospital cup she had been plied with, she hardly gave him a thought.

She didn't come across Mr Grenfell again. Once or twice she saw him, partnering the wives of other honoraries, and then with Miriam. She was a little uneasy at the manner in which she had talked to him. It was a good thing there was a round in the morning so that they could slip back into their impersonal relationship. She felt a twinge of regret at the idea, and a guilty regret too, because she and Humphrey had quarrelled on what should have been a very pleasant evening for them both. She remembered uneasily that they were to spend the next weekend with his mother; but perhaps by then Humphrey would have got over his annoyance. By the time she got into bed she was too sleepy to give much thought to it.

It had been a quiet night on the ward. Eugenia did her morning round with her usual unhurried friendliness, describing patiently to those patients well enough to be interested as many of the dresses as she could remember, handing out the post and checking, in her quiet matter-of-fact way, her patients' conditions. She had ten minutes or so in her office before the clock began to strike and she got to her feet again. It wouldn't do to keep Mr Grenfell waiting.

They met, as they always did, at the doors exactly on time, exchanged their usual polite good mornings and gathered round the first bed. Considering that the whole bunch of them had been up until the small hours, they didn't look too bad, thought Eugenia, casting surreptitious glances at her companions. True, the girl from Physiotherapy had bags under her eyes and Harry was a little pale, but Mr Grenfell looked exactly as he always did, not a well groomed hair out of place, not a speck on his well cut suit, and since his eyelids drooped over his eyes anyway, it was impossible to tell if he was tired or not. Dennis, the current houseman, looked as though he hadn't been to bed at all, although he was spruce enough. Hatty had weathered the ball very well, though. Eugenia caught her staff nurse's eye and smiled, unaware that that young lady was marvelling that Sister Smith could look so cool and composed and not in the least tired after dancing until all hours. With Mr Grenfell too, mused Hatty, and a splendid pair they had made. Sister had looked gorgeous and she had seen them laughing and talking like old friends, and here they were, back to square one, so to speak. But not permanently. The round done, coffee ordered and drunk in the office, Mr Grenfell got up to go, but at the door he paused.

'Harry, go ahead, will you—take the others with you. I'll join you on the Men's Surgical in a few minutes.'

They filed out and he closed the door behind them and then leaned against it. Eugenia watched him, listening to the familiar jingle of coins in his pocket and wondering what he had to say.

'Have you seen Humphrey?'

She said in some surprise: 'No—there's hardly been time, but I expect I shall once I'm off duty.'

He nodded. 'Good, I'm sure you'll do your utmost to patch things up. It was, after all, a silly reason to quarrel, and he's a sound young man.' He paused and stared out of the window, over her head. 'He should have a good solid future before him—you'll have security and a well ordered life and his affection.'

Eugenia stared at him round-eyed. This didn't sound like Mr Grenfell at all. Why on earth was he suddenly so concerned about her future? He had never said whether he liked Humphrey or not, but he had certainly never sung his praises in such a manner. She said uncertainly: 'Yes, I suppose I shall,' and added: 'We have a weekend free, we'll go to his mother's . . .'

Mr Grenfell straightened and put a hand on the door. 'It would be more sense if you left Mother out of it,' he said as he went away, leaving her so muddled that she sat for quite two minutes, tidying the papers on her desk over and over again and getting them into a fine mess.

She saw Humphrey that evening after supper and, mindful of Mr Grenfell's advice, told him she was sorry their quarrel had spoilt their evening. It took all her powers of persuasion to wipe the sulky look from his face, but at length her patience was rewarded and he agreed to forget the whole thing.

'You've behaved foolishly,' he pointed out in a reasonable forgiving voice, 'but we'll say no more about it, but I must ask you not to wear that flashy dress again.' He added unforgivably: 'It's not as though you're a young girl and slim.' And Eugenia, intent on pacifying him, agreed meekly, damping down the spark of anger threatening to burst into a raging inferno.

She had a busy day ahead of her. She went to sleep feeling a glow of self-satisfaction because everything was all right again and went on duty in the morning prepared to face a hard day's work and, looming near now, a weekend with her future mother-in-law.

She went home for an hour or two that evening, and sitting round the small fire with the twins on the rug and her father opposite her, she told them about the ball and touched lightly on Humphrey's displeasure. 'I had to tell him,' she explained. 'He thought I'd taken the money from my bank account.' She sighed unconsciously. 'We're both free this weekend, we're going to his mother's.'

'You will, of course, wear your new blue outfit,' advised Becky, 'and the shoes.'

Eugenia said she would; surely Humphrey, content and relaxed at his mother's home, wouldn't take exception to something as sensible as a jacket and skirt—he would probably disapprove of the shoes; low-heeled lace-ups would have longer wear in them, but after all, they were her shoes, bought with her money, and even if she loved him that was no reason to dress like a dowd. She left home with regret and the promise that she would see them all next week, and once in her room at the hospital she got out her overnight bag and packed it. She would be working until five o'clock and Humphrey didn't like to be kept waiting. There would be no time to do more than change.

CHAPTER FIVE

THE day was as busy as the previous one had been. The thoracotomy which had gone to theatre two days earlier was showing signs of congestion, so Eugenia sent for Harry and he in turn went away to fetch Mr Grenfell, who came unhurriedly, examined his patient, wrote up fresh instructions and asked that the physiotherapist should be sent for so that he might give explicit instructions about essential breathing exercises.

'I want to know of any further developments, Sister,' he told Eugenia. 'I think we've caught it in time. Anything else worrying you?'

'No, sir, thank you.'

'Good. Enjoy your weekend.'

He went quietly out of the ward again and she began on the careful task of getting the patient back on to the road to normal recovery. She was successful, she hoped, although it would fall to Hatty's lot to continue the rest of the treatment over the weekend. All the same, when she went off duty she was a little late and not quite as serene as she usually was. Humphrey would be waiting impatiently and to make matters worse she broke a finger nail, had to wait for an empty shower and laddered her tights. All the same, she regained some of her calm when she was dressed. The jacket and skirt were just right, even if she had had to wear a last year's knitted top with them, and the shoes were elegant ... She caught up her overnight bag and raced downstairs.

Humphrey was in his car, looking impatient. Eugenia got in beside him with a breathless: 'Sorry—I got held up—one of the patients.' She smiled at him and added, 'Hullo, dear.'

He pecked her cheek. 'It's a pity,' he said reasonably, 'that on the few occasions that we're able to go out together, you're invariably late.'

'Well, I can't clock-watch, can I?' she coaxed, anxious for him to be goodhumoured. 'And I'm never off duty on the dot, you know.'

He started the car and drove at a steady pace across the forecourt and into the street beyond. 'That's new—that suit you're wearing.'

'Yes.' She hoped she sounded calmer than she felt. 'I bought it with the rest of the money . . .'

'What money?' His voice was sharp.

'Well, Mrs Clarence—the patient I went to nurse in the Algarve, sent me this cheque, and since I've paid almost all of my salary into the bank this month, I spent it on clothes.'

Humphrey tightened his lips. 'Since you felt justified in doing so, I'll say no more about it.' He spoke in a reasonable voice, but she sensed that he was angry. She worked hard at getting him in a good frame of mind before they reached his mother's home, but he was still a little aloof when he stopped the car outside his home. Her heart sank as the door opened and Mrs Parsons appeared on the doorstep. She greeted her son with a wistful joy calculated to wring all but the hardest of hearts and which instantly put Eugenia's teeth on edge, then turned to her with a gushing sweetness even harder to bear.

The little lady's sharp eyes took in the whole of her person while she stooped to peck her cheek. 'New clothes?' The sweetness was tinged with acid and she gave a tinkling laugh. 'Extravagant girl, and such an expensive colour too—always at the cleaners.' Her glance fell to the shoes. 'Very smart,' her voice was suddenly plaintive. 'I only wish I could afford them, but low heels and a sensible lace-up are so much better value . . .'

Before Eugenia could answer Humphrey laughed. 'But Eugenia wasn't feeling sensible, were you, old girl?' He gave her a condescending pat on the back. 'Let's get inside, shall we?'

Mrs Parsons led the way indoors, to a house gleaming with polish, smelling faintly of pine disinfectant, and as they neared the kitchen, something roasting in the oven. 'Your favourite meal, darling,' declared that lady, opening the drawing room door. 'You come so seldom that I can afford the best of everything.' Her voice was plaintive again.

They sat in a semi-circle round an imitation coal fire with only one bar on, and presently Mrs Parsons said, as she had said a dozen times before: 'Pour us a glass of sherry, will you, darling—I save it up as a special treat for you; it's a small luxury I've had to give up since your dear father died.'

Eugenia sat, very upright so that she did not disarrange the cushions, and sipped at her sherry, listening politely to Mrs Parsons' chatter, most of it full of self-pity, handed out with an air of 'What a brave little woman I am'. She paused presently, asked perfunctorily after Eugenia's work and then listened to Humphrey's account of his busy days. Somehow, thought Eugenia, crossly, she was made to feel inferior for no reason at all; she worked as hard as Humphrey, but it was never admitted. Indeed, he made a grave reference to her visit to the Algarve, making it appear that she had had the whale of a time and mentioning the cheque, something she found hard to forgive.

'Ah,' cried Mrs Parsons playfully, 'I can see that

you're a girl who knows which side her bread is buttered!'

Eugenia's mild temper flared suddenly. 'Oh, indeed I do,' she said gently. 'Only all the butter has to go into the bank, doesn't it?'

Mrs Parsons looked affronted, observed that she would dish up their supper, and went out of the room, indignation in every line of her back.

'There was no need to be rude to Mother,' said Humphrey in the measured tones she found so hard to contradict, but just for once she was really angry.

'Then get off my back!' she snapped, and got up and went upstairs to the guest room she always slept in when she stayed the night.

It was a small room, as impersonal as a hotel bedroom and so immaculate that she was almost afraid to unpack her case. Five minutes on her own calmed her down, though, she did her face, tidied her hair and went downstairs again. Humphrey and his mother had been talking about her; she could see that from their faces, which instantly assumed expressions of innocence.

'We're waiting for you,' said Humphrey with a tolerance she didn't believe. Supper was eaten solemnly, with due regard to the perfection of Mrs Parsons' cooking and accompanied by tales of bygone comforts uttered in her wistful voice. To hear her talk, thought Eugenia, you would think she was on the breadline, and then felt ashamed for being unkind. The poor old dear must be lonely, even if she did appear to live in quite comfortable circumstances. The house was certainly much too large for her.

The evening passed as previous evenings. Eugenia had had the forethought to bring her knitting with her while she listened to mother and son talking. She was included in their conversation of course, but only from time to time, and even then she only needed to agree to what was being said.

They went to bed at a reasonable hour, with Mrs Parsons taking care that she was the last upstairs. Heaven knew what awful goings-on she imagined they would get up to, if they were left on their own, thought Eugenia naughtily—not that Humphrey was that sort of man. She sighed wistfully at the very idea.

It was wrong of her, she thought as she brushed her hair, to expect life to be more exciting. Here she was, engaged to be married, with a secure future before her, wanting something to happen. Thinking about that, she wasn't sure what.

Saturday was spent as they always spent it when they were at Mrs Parsons'—tidying the garden. When that was done they had coffee, then Humphrey got out the car and they went for what Mrs Parsons called a nice drive; round Hampstead Heath and back again to a cold lunch and a quiet afternoon, while Eugenia knitted, Mrs Parsons dozed and Humphrey read *The Times*. After tea the cards were got out and they played three-handed whist until it was time for supper; another cooked meal, concocted, if Mrs Parsons was to be believed, at great expense and trouble to herself. Eugenia, playing a careless game, sniffed the air, boiled cod and shrimp sauce.

Sunday was better. For one thing, they would go back to St Clare's after tea and church took up most of the morning. Eugenia, sitting beside Humphrey, paid no attention to the sermon at all; she was working out the next lot of off-duty in her head, wondering about the patient with the thoracotomy, and thinking, rather to her own surprise, about Mr Grenfell.

Lunch was roast beef, Yorkshire pudding and everything that went with them, followed by something out of a packet which hadn't been whipped up enough and tasted gritty. Eugenia, wiping the dishes, did her best to make conversation with Mrs Parsons while Humphrey sat in the drawing-room with the Sunday papers, for as his mother said: 'The poor boy has a heavy week's work ahead of him and needs all the rest he can get.'

Eugenia, wiping spoons and forks rather carelessly, wondered if his mother ever stopped to think that she might have a heavy week's work too. Apparently not, for, said Mrs Parsons: 'We women have no idea how hard our menfolk work to keep us in comfort.'

Eugenia murmured assent, hung the dishcloth in its appointed place and followed Mrs Parsons back into the drawing-room. There would be light conversation until teatime. She picked up her knitting, only half listening to what was being said, until it dawned upon her suddenly that Mrs Parsons was talking about their future.

'I daresay it will take me six months to sell this house,' she was saying, 'but I imagine you won't be marrying just yet. I shall sell most of the furniture, just keep enough to furnish two rooms for myself—of course I shall take my meals with you dear—so much more economical and we shall all be pleasant company for each other—besides, I shall be able to give Eugenia some cooking hints.' She beamed across at Eugenia's astounded face. 'I'm sure you've had little chance to work in a kitchen, have you, dear?'

Eugenia took a deep breath. 'As a matter of fact, I have—I can cook, too. Which is a good thing, because two women sharing a kitchen never works, does it?' She went on, pleased that her voice was so steady: 'Do you intend to live with us when we're married, Mrs Parsons?'

'Well, dear, it seems a good idea. I've given it a good deal of thought during the past few months and it has so many advantages . . .'

'Such as?'

'Company for you while Humphrey is working, and although I may not be able to do much housework—I have a very good daily woman, you know—I can advise you about so many things. I shall have my own rooms, of course.' She gave a little laugh. 'You mustn't mind if I enjoy a little privacy from time to time!'

Eugenia glanced at Humphrey and was pleased to see that he looked uncomfortable. 'You hadn't mentioned this to me,' she said quietly.

'No—well, I thought it better to wait until we could all discuss it.'

Just for the moment she had no words. She got up. 'I'll get the tea, shall I?' You won't mind if we leave earlier than usual, Mrs Parsons? Humphrey is going to drop me off at my home—I've promised to spend the evening there.'

Humphrey opened his mouth to protest, but the fierce look she gave him closed it again. He muttered something and when his mother protested said quite meekly: 'Oh, yes, I'd forgotten.'

Nothing more was said on the matter, conversation was light and impersonal and for the life of her, afterwards Eugenia couldn't remember a word of it.

In the car at last, watching Mrs Parsons being 'poor little me' as she wished Humphrey goodbye, Eugenia allowed herself to think. By the time he got in beside her and had begun the short drive back she had made at least some sense of her chaotic thoughts.

She said with dangerous calm: 'I thought that we

were saving for our own home, Humphrey, not to keep your mother in ease at our expense for the rest of her days. Because that's what it will be . . .' and when he tried to interrupt: 'No, please be quiet, it's my turn to say something. It seems to me that you and your mother have had far too much to say without including me. Your mother lives very comfortably, she has someone to do the housework—presumably,' Eugenia went on bitterly, 'she'll have me to do that when we eventually marry. There's no need for her to live with us—what kind of a life will it be? We shall never be alone.' She looked bewildered and choked with misery. 'And why couldn't you have talked about it to me? After all, I'm concerned as well, you know.'

He said stiffly: 'There's no point in discussing it while you're in this unreasonable mood, Eugenia. Later, when you've calmed down, we'll talk about it quietly.'

'I don't think it's something I can discuss quietly; at the moment I'd like to throw something at you, Humphrey! And now you can drive me to Father's house.'

Which, strangely enough, he did, without another word, waiting while she got out of the car and then driving away without a backward glance.

They were in the sitting room, her father and the twins and Plum, spending a comfortable evening spread out in front of the fire. They were surprised to see her, welcoming her with a warmth that did her chilled heart good.

Her father took off his glasses and gave her a long look. 'Had a good weekend, love?'

'No, Father.' She took off her jacket and the new shoes and curled up in the chair opposite his. 'I'd love a cup of tea . . .'

Becky got up at once. 'I'll get it, only tell me what you're going to talk about if I miss anything.'

Eugenia found it difficult to start, but once she had there was no stopping her, and at the end she asked: 'What am I to do, Father? It won't work, having Mrs Parsons to live with us. She doesn't like me, and I'll be honest and say that I don't like her—I mean not in the way I should like a mother-in-law.' She heaved an indignant breath. 'Besides, why should I save every penny I can spare to furnish a house for her to live in?' She paused. 'Well, no—not quite that. She said she'd bring her own furniture with her, but she wants to teach me how to cook . . .'

'You cook beautifully,' protested Bruce, and Becky, pouring the tea, said: 'Don't marry Humphrey, Eugenia.'

'An easy way out,' agreed Mr Smith, 'but perhaps not the right one. I agree that the whole thing is most unsatisfactory, but there's one thing you've forgotten, my dear. You don't plan to get married for another two years, do you? In that time Mrs Parsons might remarry, she might—forgive me for saying so—die. Humphrey might realise that it wouldn't work, that he wants a home of his own. Do nothing, love, say nothing, let the whole thing fade into vagueness.'

Which Eugenia did, although it cost her something to meet Humphrey the next day and have to behave as though nothing had happened. She had spent a poor night, brooding over the future, so that she was a little pale in the morning, a fact which Mr Grenfell noted without comment. Instead he enquired politely if she had enjoyed her weekend, in exactly the same manner as he had for the last three years, and then gone about the business of the round with his usual calm manner. But unusually, he made no comment about Humphrey as they drank their coffee afterwards; normally he would make some polite reference to him, but today he kept the conversation strictly impersonal, even chilly. Eugenia, who had come to enjoy his more friendly manner, saw him go with peevish regret. It would have been very comforting to have told him all about Mrs Parsons, even asked his advice, but his austere manner had precluded that. She sighed and went into the ward; there was a new student nurse to be shown the ropes. The girl, small and pretty and a little scared of the underwater drainage jars under the beds and the variety of drips scattered around, needed a friendly helping hand until she found her way about.

Eugenia had had to look for Humphrey after she went off duty. From long experience she knew that after a tiff she would have to be the one to make up; once she had done so, then he would be magnanimous and everything would be all right between them. But although she apologised for losing her temper with him, she would say nothing about his mother coming to live with them; let him be the first to bring the subject up, and since it was obvious that he had no intention of doing that for the moment, the subject was pushed into an uneasy background.

All the same, as the days slid by, the uneasiness and uncertainty stayed at the back of her head. If she didn't talk about it to someone she would burst, and since Mr Grenfell was maintaining his polite indifference, she decided to go home one evening. It was hardly the weather in which to go out; it had been drizzling all day and now the rain was coming down in earnest and a cutting wind had sprung up. London looked muddy and drab, especially the crowded streets round the hospital. Eugenia took her place at the end of a long queue for the bus. It was short-tempered to boot, for apparently, as so often happened, there wasn't a bus in sight and everyone was becoming wetter by the minute and impatient to the point of ill-temper. Eugenia, at the tail end, shivered. Her raincoat wasn't quite waterproof any more; if she had been a sensible girl she should have bought a new one instead of squandering her money on a dress she would probably not wear again until it was out of date . . .

The woman behind her prodded her with her umbrella and uttered a surly 'Sorry', and a car, travelling fast, splashed muddy water on to her legs. Perhaps it would be a good idea to call off her evening at home and go back to the hospital to a hot bath and bed. She was summoning the energy to do this when she was aware of a car drawing in to the pavement and its door opening. 'Get in,' said Mr Grenfell.

Rain or no rain, she wasn't in the mood to be ordered about. 'I'm going home,' she told him.

'Get in! I'll take you.'

'Oh, get in, do,' begged the woman behind her. 'Some of us don't know a good thing when we see it!'

Eugenia got in. 'Well, really, Mr Grenfell,' she began, to be halted by his, 'Gerard—I thought we'd agreed to that.' He wormed the car between traffic. 'Where to— no, don't tell me . . . ninety-six, Trafalgar Street, Islington.'

'How did you know?' and then: 'I'm dripping all over your beautiful car!'

'It is raining,' he pointed out reasonably. 'Harry told me.'

'Well, I must say! Why . . .?'

'I really can't remember.' His voice was casual. 'You've had a busy day, haven't you?'

They talked shop comfortably in a friendly way until he stopped in front of her home. Eugenia prepared to get out. 'Thank you for the lift—I hope I haven't taken you out of your way?'

It amazed her that a self-assured man could look so utterly lonely. 'I wasn't going anywhere,' he told her, and rather against her better judgment she said:

'Well, would you like to come in for a cup of coffee?'

The gleam in his eyes was hidden by their lids. 'Why, yes, that would be very delightful—if I'm not going to be in the way.'

'Heavens, no!' said Eugenia cheerfully. 'The twins have friends walking in and out all the time.'

'The twins?'

'Brother and sister, Becky and Bruce. She opened her door. 'They're not expecting me, so I daresay the place will be in a fearful state.'

He smiled. 'Oh, do you descend upon them at intervals and put things to rights?'

'Not really—when I'm at home I cook and so on, but they manage very well.'

She led the way up the short path to the front door and turned the handle. It was warm indoors and there was a smell of toast coming from the kitchen at the back of the narrow hall.

'It's me!' called Eugenia as she peeled off her wet mac and opened the sitting-room door. She was met by the twins, rushing at her with delighted cries. 'Just in time to help me with my maths!' cried Bruce, and was pushed aside by Becky. 'No, me first,' she cried. 'There's this about Charles the First and you were always good at History and Father is busy with a book he found today . . .'

They slithered to a halt at the sight of Mr Grenfell, towering in the doorway, but before Eugenia could speak, Bruce said; 'You're Mr Grenfell—I'd have known you anywhere.'

'A compliment, I feel sure, but why?' He offered a large hand.

'Well, Eugenia's described you. I'll take your coat, it's wet.'

Eugenia's colour had heightened. 'Where's Father, my dears?'

'In the kitchen. We've got our homework to do, so he said he'd get the supper.'

Mr Smith wandered in, spoon in hand. He said happily: 'Ah, Eugenia, just in time, my dear—I've been scrambling eggs, but somehow they don't look right.' He peered over his glasses at Mr Grenfell, standing imperturbably behind Eugenia. 'Ah, Mr Grenfell, is it not? I'm delighted to meet you. Come in and join us for supper. I'm sure Eugenia will be able to find something for us to eat.'

Eugenia cast her parent a look of loving exasperation. 'I expect Mr Grenfell——' she began, and was brought to a halt by his voice. 'I should very much like to have supper with you,' he observed equably. 'I have wanted to make your acquaintance, Mr Smith. Eugenia mentioned once that you're interested in rare books. I have a small library of first editions . . .'

Eugenia cast him a look of suspicious enquiry, but he wasn't looking at her. The twins had drawn up an armchair to the small fire, and he and her father had plunged instantaneously into talk. She went into the kitchen, turned off the grill, removed the burnt toast under it, scraped the contents of a saucepan into the waste bucket and started on the supper. Scrambled eggs, she decided, her pretty nose in and out of the cupboards, buttered toast, baked beans and a small dish of left-over potatoes she could turn into french fries. There would be no pudding, but she would make coffee and there was plenty of cheese. She found some crackers, slapped butter into a dish and went through into the dining room to lay the table.

Becky joined her. 'I'll do this,' she volunteered. 'I'm stuck with Charles the First anyway. Isn't he smashing?'

'Yes, love, quite nice.' Eugenia looked at her younger sister helplessly. 'But I never meant him to come to supper.'

'Why not? I daresay he's hungry,' said the practical Becky. 'When he and Father stop talking I shall ask him to give me a hand with the kings of England.'

Eugenia went back to the kitchen and started to cook. She did it well, and the dishes she put on the table presently looked appetising; she doubted if Mrs Parsons could have done better. She poked her head round the sitting-room door and said: 'Supper,' and then: 'Bring your beer with you, it'll get cold if you don't come now.'

It was surprising how easily Mr Grenfell had slipped into the family circle. The Smiths were great talkers and it seemed, to Eugenia's astonishment, that he was too. The conversation, completely taken up with first editions, the Stuart Kings, and Pythagoras, flowed easily, she had little to do but pile plates with food, pour coffee and utter a word or two when appealed to from time to time.

'A delightful meal,' declared Mr Grenfell, finally. 'Humphrey has got himself a Cordon Bleu cook. I can't think why,' he went on deliberately, 'he hasn't snapped you up before now,' and at her outraged look: 'Oh, I'm aware that you're saving for the ideal home, whatever that is, but no amount of kitchen gadgets will make up for a well scrambled egg.' His glance gathered agreement from his companions. 'Think of the fun you'll have, dishing up a tasty supper for him when he gets home after a hard day's work.'

It was Becky who said suddenly: 'His mother's going to live with them.' Mr Grenfell's eyelids dropped even lower. He appeared not to notice the furious look Eugenia cast at her young sister.

'Becky, have you finished your homework?'

Becky gave her an innocent look. 'Oh yes, Eugenia, Mr Grenfell helped me. If you want to talk I'll wash up and Bruce can dry.'

Mr Grenfell pushed back his chair. 'Supposing I help you, Becky? I daresay Eugenia would like to talk to her father before we go back.'

'A very decent sort of chap,' declared Mr Smith from his chair by the sitting room fire. 'I daresay he's never washed a dish in his life.'

'Probably not,' agreed Eugenia tartly. 'Father, whatever possessed Becky to say that? It's none of Mr Grenfell's business . . .'

'In that case, my dear, there's no harm done,' muttered her parent, 'he'll probably forget it. He's going to be married himself, I believe?'

'Did he tell you that?' She wondered why she felt so unhappy at the news—after all, she had known about his engagement since before Christmas. 'She's like a model; very slim and dresses beautifully . . .'

Her father ignored this. 'Is that why you came home, love? To talk to us about Mrs Parsons? I must say I don't think it will do at all—have you seen Humphrey?'

'Yes—and I did as you suggested; it wasn't mentioned. Perhaps it'll turn out all right.' She sounded very uncertain. 'Father, I don't think I could bear to have her living with us . . .'

'That rather depends on how much you love Humphrey, my dear.'

'Well, of course I love him—we're engaged . . .' She added a little desperately: 'If only we could get married and not have to wait!'

Her father didn't say anything to that, and she looked at him enquiringly.

'Don't you agree, Father?'

'He didn't answer, because the door opened and the twins and Mr Grenfell came in, obviously on the best of terms. 'I must be going,' said Eugenia briskly, 'and don't bother to drive me back, Mr Grenfell, there's a bus stop just down the road.'

He was as bad as her father, ignoring her remarks. 'Get your coat, then, and we'll be off.' He shook Mr Smith's hand. 'A delightful evening,' he observed. 'I hope you'll invite me again. I hope you've no objection to the twins coming to see me. My dog's just had pups; I know they can't have one—Plum wouldn't like it, would he?' He put out a finger to tickle the little cat's head. 'But they're charming little creatures at the moment, and Bruce and Becky might like to look them over.' He glanced across at Eugenia. 'On your next day off, perhaps?'

Eugenia, feeling cornered, opened her mouth to refuse; her father, closely echoed by the twins, said immediately: 'What a splendid idea—we can't keep a dog here, of course; if we're ever able to live in the country again . . .' He didn't finish the sentence. There was very little hope of that; he wasn't young any more; soon he would retire on a small pension and it would be harder than ever to keep the twins going until they were educated—decently educated so that they could get jobs in some profession or other. Even with scholarships and grants when available it would take some doing.

Eugenia watched him, knowing exactly what he was thinking. She said cheerfully: 'What a splendid idea! I shall like that—it's half term next week, isn't it?'

'Wednesday,' said Bruce. 'Gerard says you're free then, and so are we.'

'We'll settle the details later,' murmured Mr Grenfell, not giving her a chance to say a word.

In the car she made an effort to assert herself. 'I'm not sure about Wednesday,' she began, and was instantly pounced upon with his:

'You had other plans? What are they? Can't they be put off? Humphrey is on call, isn't he, and since it isn't pay day for another ten days I don't imagine you'll be going shopping.'

'I don't have to tell you how I spend my off-duty,' she declared with a snap.

'Of course not, but it would be a pity to disappoint Becky and Bruce, wouldn't it? I'll pick you up about two o'clock and we can collect them both on the way.'

She made a last feeble effort. 'I don't know where you live . . .'

'Well, if you come on Wednesday you soon will, won't you?' said Mr Grenfell blandly.

Eugenia met Humphrey the next morning, on her way to the Office to ask for a nurse to cover Nurse Sims, who'd gone off sick. He stood in front of her, smiling. 'And where were you yesterday evening?' he wanted to know jovially. 'I had an hour or so to spare and thought we might have had a drink.'

'I went home.' She had blushed quite guiltily and he looked at her with approval, thinking she was blushing at meeting him unexpectedly.

'They're all well?' he asked. Eugenia had known since their engagement that he was ill at ease with her father, and had very little time for the twins, so she didn't enlarge on her: 'Fine, thanks. Are you busy?'

'My dear girl, I'm always up to my eyes. What about you, taking a stroll before your coffee break?'

Why had she never found it irritating until now—the way he pretended she did no work? And yet he must know that she did—she held down an exacting job, and without being conceited about it, she was aware that she gave full value for her salary. She said lightly: 'I had coffee hours ago and I'm on my way to the Office.' She smiled at him. 'See you around.'

He caught her arm as she turned to go. 'Hey, not so fast! I'm free for a couple of hours on Wednesday afternoon—it's your day off . . .'

'Yes, I know. I'm sorry, Humphrey, I promised I'd take the twins out—it's half term, you know.'

'Oh, well,' he was irritated because he couldn't have his own way, 'we'll get together some time.'

She hurried away with a quick backward smile, feeling quite guilty again; although there was no reason why she shouldn't tell him that she would be seeing Mr Grenfell—after all, the twins would be there.

It rained on and off for the next few days, and Eugenia had resigned herself to wearing her raincoat and sensible shoes; not that it mattered in the least what she would wear, she reminded herself. It was, after all, only Mr Grenfell, who actually never looked at her. At least, she amended, not often.

But on Wednesday morning when she woke up, it was to see the sun shining from a blue sky—splendid April weather and all the more delightful because it came so seldom. She would be able to wear the blue jacket and skirt after all, and her new shoes. Heaven send an uneventful morning so that she would get off duty promptly.

Heaven, it seemed, was on her side. She left the ward barely ten minutes late, skipped her dinner, made tea in the home while she showered and changed and presented herself, nicely made up and not a hair out of place only five minutes after two o'clock in the car park, where Mr Grenfell lounged in the Bentley.

He got out long before she reached him and opened the door for her. His, 'Hullo, Eugenia,' was urbane, as was his careless, 'A quiet morning?'

'Oh, yes—very.' She hopped into the car and glowed at his pleasant, 'That's a nice thing you're wearing.' His gaze swept down to her feet. 'You should wear high heels more often.'

'If I did, I'd have to lean over everyone to talk to them!'

'Not me, you wouldn't,' he said cheerfully. 'You've had lunch?'

She said far too quickly: 'Yes, thanks,' and thought of the half-eaten biscuit and the mug of tea. But what did lunch matter at the moment? It struck her forcibly that when she went out with Humphrey he usually suggested that she should have a meal first, for, as she jokingly put it, it was a pity to miss a meal she had paid for, and half an hour, more or less didn't really matter. But now it was a glorious day and the sun was shining, she was sitting in a super car, and she had to admit that Mr Grenfell's company was always stimulating.

She voiced her thoughts: 'This is really very nice, and it's such a heavenly day too.' She gave a happy sigh. 'I love April.'

The calm expression on her companion's face didn't alter. 'I must agree, but I think I'll wait for May.'

She turned a puzzled face to his. 'Why do you say that?'

'Somebody—Edward Way Teale, I think—wrote "All things seem possible in May".'

She was just as puzzled. 'Oh, are you—that is, do you plan to get married then?'

He said gravely: 'You take the very words from my mouth, Eugenia.'

For some reason she felt depressed. Mr Grenfell's

choice of a wife was his own business, of course, but she couldn't help feeling that if he married Miriam he would be making the mistake of a lifetime. It was a pity she didn't know him well enough to tell him so.

The streets were fairly quiet and the twins were ready and waiting by the time they reached her home. Rather to her surprise Mr Grenfell elected to go in with her, although her father wasn't at home. She discovered why when she saw him laying a book on the sitting room table. 'For your father—he mentioned that he was looking for a copy, and I happened to have one at home.'

He stood patiently tickling Plum's furry head while Becky made a last-minute search for her purse, and then he ushered his party outside and into the car. This time Eugenia shared the back seat with Becky while Bruce sat beside Mr Grenfell, beginning on a string of questions which lasted as they went through the streets once more, in the direction of the river this time, with the streets and houses becoming larger and wider until they turned into Fulham Road and then the King's Road and finally into Cheyne Walk.

Becky bounced forward and poked her face over Mr Grenfell's shoulder. 'I say, you don't live here, do you, Gerard?' she wanted to know excitedly.

He half turned his head to smile at her. 'Indeed I do.' He slowed the car and stopped before a Georgian terrace house, separated from the pavement by an iron railing and a small garden. It had a wide porch and sash windows rising in four neat rows to its roof, and as they got out of the car, Eugenia glanced over her shoulder; the view of the Thames and Battersea Park took her breath, before she turned back to the house. Not at all the kind of home she had expected Mr Grenfell to have. Vaguely, she had imagined that he lived in a service flat in one of the great faceless blocks convenient to St Clare's. But of course, she reminded herself, if he was going to get married soon, he would need a house. Miriam, she guessed, wouldn't be happy in anything else. Probably she had chosen this one and furnished it . . .

She was mistaken. She heard him answer some question of Becky's: 'My family have lived here for a very long time—it's too big at present, but I wouldn't want to live anywhere else.'

A remark which cheered her up considerably, although she wasn't quite sure why.

CHAPTER SIX

MR GRENFELL ushered his small party along the short path, unlocked his front door and stood aside for them to go in, at the same time giving a piercing whistle, instantly answered by a loud barking. A moment later a door at the back of the square hall swung violently open to admit a portly golden labrador, who in her turn was followed by an equally portly man, no longer young, but very spruce in his dark suit.

'This is Pringle,' said Mr Grenfell. 'He and Mrs Pringle look after me—Pringle, this is Miss Smith and Becky and Bruce Smith.' He stood fondling the dog's head while they shook hands. 'And this is Muffin.'

They greeted the dog suitably while Pringle relieved the twins of their coats. 'Very glad to see you, she is,' he observed. 'Looking forward to a bit of a ramble in the garden.'

'A garden here?' asked Eugenia.

'Oh, quite a large one. There's even a small wood at the end of it. Would you like to see the puppies first or shall we take Muffin for a stroll?'

'The puppies,' chorused the twins, 'please!'

The small creatures were curled up in a large basket in the kitchen, a splendidly equipped room which somehow managed to look comfortably old-fashioned. And the short, stout little lady standing at the kitchen table, floury arms in a bowl of dough, looked the same. 'Mrs Pringle,' said Mr Grenfell, 'my housekeeper. Miss Smith, Becky, and Bruce Smith.'

'Pleased, I'm sure,' chuckled Mrs Pringle. 'Excuse me if I don't shake hands, I'd spoil the pastry.'

'God forbid,' observed Mr Grenfell seriously, and led the way to the puppies.

There was a tabby cat sitting with them. 'My Maudie,' said Mrs Pringle. 'Kind of nursemaid, she is, when Muffin's not there. Thinks they're kittens, I daresay.'

They spent some time kneeling by the basket while Muffin stood by her master, occasionally bending to snuff gently at her puppies, while Maudie slept peacefully. 'I'd love to have one,' said Becky longingly, 'but of course we can't, not in our little house—now if we were back at Chilcoate Magna . . .'

Eugenia frowned. She didn't think, as far as she could remember, that she had ever mentioned her old home to Mr Grenfell; for some reason she didn't bother to think about, she didn't want him to know about it. She said hastily: 'Yes—well, love, we really can't have a puppy, can we? There'd be no one at home to look after him—he's far happier here.'

Mr Grenfell made no comment, merely remarking that if they had looked their fill, they might like to go round the garden.

A quite large garden. Walking down its well kept paths, it was possible to forget that London was all round them; it had been cleverly screened by a variety of trees and shrubs and there were spring flowers all over the place. And when they reached the end there was the bluebell wood; small but genuine. Eugenia stopped in her tracks and drew in a fragrant breath.

'It's heavenly! However did you manage it, right in the middle of all these streets and houses?'

'I think it was because of the streets and houses that my father planted it.'

'Oh,' she looked at him in surprise, 'have you always lived here?'

'All my life.' There was content and satisfaction in his voice and she said: 'You must love it very much,' and then in a sudden burst of frankness: 'I always thought of you as living in a service flat.'

'But then you know so little about me, Eugenia.'

Becky and Bruce were at the other end of the little wood with Muffin, she could hear their happy voices, and just for the moment she wished with all her heart that she could call a halt to time and stay there in the sunshine with the bluebells all around her and the thin evening light dappling the trees. Such thoughts were nonsense, of course, and disloyal to Humphrey. She gave an involuntary shudder at a mental picture of a semi-detached in one of the better suburbs, well maintained, because Humphrey wouldn't settle for anything less, its garden neat and uninspired and not a blade of grass out of place; certainly not a bluebell in sight . . .

'Will you stay for tea?' asked Mr Grenfell, gently cutting across her thoughts.

They had their tea in a sitting room at the back of the house with french windows opening on to the garden, sandwiches cut paper-thin, tiny cakes and a large chocolate cake oozing cream. Becky and Bruce tucked in with uninhibited pleasure, while Eugenia nibbled at the sandwiches and looked around her. The room was delightfully furnished with two large sofas covered in tawny velvet, one each side of a small fireplace, a modicum of lamps on tables, and a scattering of small comfortable chairs covered in paler shades of velvet. The floor was covered by a Turkey carpet, its various colours pleasantly dimmed by age.

'You like it?' asked Mr Grenfell suddenly.

'Very much.' She tried to think of something else to say and couldn't. Singularly stupid of her to feel shy—after all, she had known him for three years or more and had never once felt anything else but professional interest in his remarks. She busied herself refilling his cup and hoped he would embark on some general topic. But it seemed that he wasn't going to, and when she glanced at him presently, it was to find him watching her. When he did speak, it was to take her quite by surprise.

'Your home at Chilcoate Magna—it had a garden?'

'Yes. As big as this one, but not nearly so well planned.'

'And the house?' he persisted gently.

She shot a frustrated glance at Becky, whose fault it was that he knew anything about it, anyway. 'Oh, just a country house on the edge of the village.'

'You must miss it.'

Before she could reply Becky chimed in: 'Oh, she does—we all do, but we had to move. We pretend that we don't mind living in Islington, but as soon as Bruce and I have got ourselves educated we plan to buy it back.'

'A most salutory aim,' remarked Mr Grenfell, and looked so encouraging that Becky had her mouth open to tell him even more, only Eugenia stopped her in time by remarking on the beauty of the tapestry firescreen.

Mr Grenfell's mouth twitched, but he agreed with her politely, in fact, enlarged upon its history at some length, and by the time he had finished, Eugenia was able to suggest that it was time, she felt, they should go home.

'And please don't bother to see us home,' she begged him. 'I'm sure there's a bus close by.'

He had got out of his chair to shut the french

window. 'I have to go back to St Clare's,' he told her
smoothly, 'and Muffin is longing for a ride. I've no
doubt Maudie will keep an eye on the puppies till we
get back.'

It would have been ungracious to have protested
further, so they bade the Pringles goodbye and went
back down the short path and got into the car. When
they were almost at the hospital Eugenia said stiffly:
'Thank you for a pleasant afternoon, Mr Grenfell. It
was great fun, and the bluebell wood was something to
remember. If you'd like to drop us off here we can
easily catch a bus . . .'

'So very anxious to be rid of me, Eugenia,' he said
softly. 'I wonder why? I need only leave a note for
Harry with the porter on duty. Wait in the car, will
you?'

He didn't stop to see if she agreed, but whisked
himself out of his seat and in through the hospital
doors, to reappear in a very short time indeed.

'Oh, good,' said Bruce. 'You're coming back with
us—Father will be pleased. When Eugenia's home we
usually have coffee and cake before she goes back. Will
you stop and have some too?'

Eugenia felt indignation rise within her as Mr
Grenfell, without even bothering to look at her, agreed.
Anyway, he wouldn't stay long; he would most
certainly have some date or other during the evening,
and even if he hadn't, he wouldn't want to miss his
dinner.

She was quite wrong. He went into the house with
them, spent half an hour with her father, helped Bruce
with his biology and then settled down to coffee and
cake and a pleasant evening round the small fire. It was
Becky who asked suddenly: 'Do you mind missing your
dinner? It's after eight o'clock. We have dinner in the

middle of the day and so does Father—Eugenia cooks when she's at home. I could cut some sandwiches for you?'

'You're very kind, Becky, but I—er—had a splendid meal at midday myself, and this cake is delicious.'

'Eugenia made it. She makes one every week. I suppose when she marries Humphrey she won't be able to . . .'

'Well, they won't get married for ages, so you'll be able to cook yourself by then,' observed her brother.

The conversation, Eugenia thought, was getting altogether too personal. She made a crisp remark about the weather and Mr Grenfell followed her at once, proving, she told herself, that he found such family gossip boring.

But if he did, he concealed it well. It was another two hours before he got up to go, with the twins on the verge of going to their beds, urging him to come again, echoed by their father, too. But not by Eugenia.

He thanked them, observing that he wouldn't want to encroach on any visit Humphrey would make.

'Oh, but he almost never comes,' said Becky. 'He doesn't like us, and he never knows what to say to Father.'

'That will do, Becky!' Eugenia's voice was sharp. And as Mr Grenfell turned his thoughtful gaze upon her flushed face: 'Of course we shall be delighted to see you whenever you can come, Mr Grenfell—though I don't suppose,' she added ingenuously, 'that will be often, you must have a great many friends.'

'One always finds time for friends,' drawled Mr Grenfell, at his most bland.

They drove back in almost total silence while Eugenia tried to think of something to say. Why, she wondered, was light conversation so difficult with him? She mumbled a few commonplaces, and felt relief as he stopped the car before the hospital entrance. 'It's been very nice,' she told him hurriedly. 'Thank you very much,' and put her hand on the door, to have it covered at once by his large one.

'Does it strike you that this is becoming a little monotonous—I've given up the habit of counting the number of times you've offered thanks before bolting away like a startled rabbit. There are other ways, you know.'

She gave her hand an experimental wriggle and felt his clasp tighten. She should feel angry, but she didn't. Instead she felt pleasantly excited, not at all how she should feel; an engaged girl with a faithful Humphrey somewhere on the other side of the door, probably hard at it on the wards. And Mr Grenfell should know better. What would Miriam think?—not that Eugenia cared about that. She said clearly in what she hoped was her usual pleasantly cool voice: 'Humphrey would have loved your garden, Mr Grenfell.'

He took his hand away at once. 'A keen gardener?' he asked, his voice as mild as milk. 'I must ask him round one day, it might inspire him to start a bluebell wood of his own.'

He got out of the car and came round to open her door. 'Goodnight, Eugenia; a very pleasant day.'

Eugenia went through the hospital and up to her room and undressed slowly. She was in bed when she remembered that Humphrey had been free that afternoon and she hadn't even thought about him once. She turned over and closed her eyes, intent on getting to sleep. She would ask him when he would be free again and be sure to see that she would be likewise.

He was free the very next evening, and so was she. They had had a hard day behind them, and Eugenia for one was feeling guilty as well as tired. She had argued with herself all day that she should tell him about her afternoon with the twins; that it should be perfectly easy to do so, but she had shrunk from the controlled annoyance he would show, his handsome features rigid with displeased hurt. But in any case, she had had no chance to say anything, because he didn't mention the matter at all, being quite taken up with a lengthy diatribe concerning a difficult diagnosis he had made that morning. She ate her chicken in a basket and drank the beer she had been given and which she disliked, and listened, trying to take an interest, her tired mind wanting nothing more than to stop thinking for a while. When Humphrey paused to take a mouthful of chips, she said: 'I've had a busy day, too, Humphrey.'

'Yes,' his interest was transitory, 'you've got plenty of staff, haven't you? I suppose Grenfell takes advantage of his seniority.'

She said seriously: 'Oh, I don't think so; it would be a difficult ward to manage unless we had sufficient nurses, and some of them are very junior and need a lot of teaching.'

Humphrey took a pull at his beer. 'Well, as I was saying, this case of mine—I knew it wasn't a normal polyneuritis—the paralysis was there, but there was a degree of fever and severe headache . . .'

Eugenia allowed her thoughts to wander hazily. Presently she said abruptly: 'Why does your mother want to come and live with us when we get married, Humphrey?'

He took a mouthful of chicken very deliberately. 'You have no interest in my work—probably you're tired. I suggest some sort of tonic to give you more stamina. This is certainly no time to discuss our future, Eugenia.'

'Why not?'

He laughed indulgently. 'It's obvious that your mind isn't clear.' He patted her arm. 'Never mind—I've got a surprise for you. I've got hold of a couple of tickets for that new show at the Prince of Wales. Next Saturday, so fix your off-duty, will you?'

'Humphrey, how super! They must have cost the earth.'

'As a matter of fact, they're complimentary—stalls.'

'Well, I'm on duty until eight o'clock, but I'll get Hatty to change with me.' She added, half laughing: 'Mind you, if there's a flap on, I'll have to stay.'

'Rubbish, darling, you're not indispensable, you know.'

'No, but I can be an extra pair of hands when they're needed.'

He finished his chicken and leant over the table to take her hand. 'I can't imagine anything much happening on a weekend—no theatre and all the Tuesday cases out of the wood. Besides, Hatty is pretty good, isn't she?'

'Splendid.' She didn't add that at the weekends they were pretty thin on the ground for those very reasons.

They strolled back to St Clare's in harmony, and Eugenia, relieved to have Humphrey so goodhumoured, didn't bring up the subject of his mother again.

In bed later, she accused herself of being a coward and then took comfort from her father's advice that she should do nothing for the time being. And Humphrey was right, of course. Weekends were usually just the routine business.

Humphrey couldn't always be right, though. She was on the point of giving the report to Hatty before going off duty when the phone rang. The Accident Room; Eugenia felt a horrible premonition shoot through her before anyone spoke.

'It's me, Laura,' and one of Eugenia's closest friends in charge of the Accident Room. 'I say, love, you've got a load of trouble coming your way. A nasty smash in the Old Kent Road; we've got them sorted out and you'll be getting three. Stove-in chest—she was driving and took the full force of the wheel; a nasty penetrating wound and a collapse of the left lung, and a small girl, who got shot on to some railings and was impaled. They'll be up in fifteen minutes.'

Eugenia said, 'Thanks,' automatically, repeated the whole story and then started giving orders. 'There's one empty bed, get the student nurse to open it up. Get Nurse Sims to get Mrs Brown and Miss Phipps out of their beds and settled in chairs—she can strip the beds and make them up, but don't let her forget to clean them down first. Get the trolleys out, will you? Then pop down to Women's Medical and see if they'll take Mrs Brown and Miss Phipps for the night.' She added thoughtfully: 'Can we manage with four, Hatty?'

'You're off duty, Sister.'

'Well, I was, but I'm not now. Nip off, Hatty, and do your stuff; I'll do some phoning.'

Routine calls to the office, the Path Lab., X-ray, the porters, and since she had made them so many times quickly dealt with.

They were ready when they brought the first case in; a youngish woman with all the signs and symptoms of haemothorax, and only semi-conscious. Eugenia, casting a careful eye over her, knew that she would need surgery urgently to evacuate the blood in her chest, endorsed by Harry coming hard on the heels of the stretcher. 'Mr Grenfell's on his way,' he told her. 'They're getting Theatre ready now—they'll have to use the other two theatres as well, but these three are the most urgent.'

Eugenia, busy making out a chart, nodded. 'Pre-med?' she asked.

It was Mr Grenfell who answered her, very correct in a dinner jacket and not looking in the least like a surgeon. Poor Miriam, thought Eugenia, and handed him the chart.

'Shall we have a look?' He glanced at Harry. 'I took a quick look at the others downstairs; I think this one needs surgery at once—then the little girl. I want all three in Intensive Care afterwards; they can be warded as soon as I say so. Sister . . .' He issued a string of instructions in his quiet voice, and she answered him just as quietly and then set about carrying them out. She was supervising the admission of the little girl when the phone rang. There was no one to answer it until Mr Grenfell, on his way across the ward, went through to the office.

When he came back he joined her by the child's bedside. 'It was for you, Sister. You are, I believe, off duty?'

She had quite forgotten Humphrey. 'Rubbish,' she said tartly. 'How could I possibly go off duty now? We're short-staffed as it is.'

He grunted softly to himself and bent over his small patient. 'Not as bad as I'd feared,' he said at length. 'Four penetrating wounds, but as far as I can see none of them have pierced anything really vital. I'll have her up next, please. The haemothorax shouldn't take too long.' He looked round. 'There's another woman . . .'

'Coming in now,' said Eugenia calmly.

'Ah yes—the pneumothorax. I'll have to do an exploration; it's impossible to assess the damage at the moment.'

He got up and went over to the bed with Harry beside him. 'A small wound too. She's very cyanosed

and dyspnoea is severe, isn't it?' He straightened his
great body. 'Right, Sister, Harry will write up the pre-
meds, I'll have them up in the order in which I saw
them, but give them all at the same time. The first one
won't be of much use, but we can't afford to wait.' He
nodded and went away with Harry at his heels, leaving
Eugenia with her hands full. The pre-meds, identification
bracelets, gowns to be put on, porters to send for. She
sent Harry to Theatre with the first case, and set about
preparing the little girl. She had almost finished when
Humphrey came into the ward.

He came and stood at the foot of the bed, ignoring
Nurse Sims on the other side. 'You're off duty,' he said,
and she could hear the anger in his voice. 'We're due at
the theatre in exactly half an hour.'

'Don't bother me now,' said Eugenia. 'Can't you see
how busy we are? There's been a major road accident. I
can't leave.' She bent to adjust the identity bracelet
round the young arm. 'Why not take your mother?'

She didn't wait for an answer as she arranged the
theatre pack over the girl on the bed. 'Nurse Sims,
you'll take this case up to Theatre, please. Staff Nurse
will relieve you just as soon as I can spare her.'

She didn't notice Humphrey turn on his heel and go
out of the ward. The first case came back and the girl
took her place, and an hour later the last case was sent
for. The night staff were on by now, carrying on with
their usual evening chores, settling patients for the
night, taking round drinks, giving out sleeping tablets.
The girl wouldn't be back until the morning; she would
spend the night in intensive care, but the first case
hadn't been as bad as they had expected. All the same,
she was ill and Eugenia, in conference with the Surgical
Night Sister, arranged for a nurse to special her until
morning. It was getting on for eleven o'clock by the

time the third case came back. It had proved a tricky business dealing with her collapsed lung and exploring the wound, but at least she was out of danger.

The night staff had taken over by now. Eugenia had stayed on, as relations of the patients had arrived; they had to be talked to, listened to with a sympathetic ear and given tea with her reassurances, while they waited to see Mr Grenfell.

He came presently, his hands in his pockets, jingling the loose change there, not a hair out of place. Eugenia, conscious of a shining face and untidy hair, wondered how he did it as she ushered them in turn into the office. Now she could surely go, she decided. Night Sister was back again, the extra nurse had arrived, and there was really nothing more that she could do. She was whispering goodnight to her colleague when she heard Mr Grenfell's voice, not loud but very clear.

He glanced up as she put her head around the door. 'I shall want to see you before you go off, Sister—if you'd be so good as to wait.'

Nicely put, as polite as ever, but she was hungry and it was long past bedtime. She murmured, withdrew her head and catching Night Sister's eye, cast her own beautiful ones up to the ceiling.

The junior nurse was having trouble with Mrs Bragg, a wilful old lady of eighty-odd, who had taken it into her head to get out of bed in search of a meal. Eugenia joined the two ladies, the one so old and the other so young, lifted her patient back into bed and tucked her in carefully. 'Just you wait a minute, Mrs Bragg,' she whispered. 'Nurse will get you a nice cup of tea and a few slices of bread and butter. It's a bit late for supper and far too early for breakfast.'

She glanced at the nurse, who went silently down the ward to the kitchen, to reappear with commendable speed with a tray. She had added jam to the bread and butter; the girl would go far, thought Eugenia, and nodded approval before going soundlessly back towards her office. Mr Grenfell must surely be ready soon.

He was, in fact, ushering the last of the relatives out of the office and across the landing to the lifts. He glanced at Eugenia as she got near him. 'Sister, could you spare a nurse for a moment to show Mr and Mrs Weldon to the rest room? They would like to stay the night——'

She went over to the nurse specialling the first case, whispered instructions, and took her place. Another five minutes more or less would make no difference now; it would be a short night. Eugenia thought fleetingly of their spoilt theatre outing; there wouldn't be another one to take its place, either. Complimentary tickets were rare these days, and Humphrey wouldn't waste money on them. She sighed, unaware that Mr Grenfell had come to stand just behind her. She started when he said quietly: 'She'll do—it's the girl I'm worried about. Why are you here?'

'You wanted a nurse to show the Weldons to the rest room; there's no one to spare.'

He didn't answer but bent to examine his patient, and presently went away, about to see Night Sister who was checking medicines at the drug cupboard.

The nurse came back and Eugenia stifled a yawn, wished her goodnight and went across the ward. She smiled at her friend, and muttered woodenly: 'You wanted me, Mr Grenfell.'

His hooded eyes examined her tired, lovely face. 'Indeed, yes.' His voice was very quiet and so bland that she wondered what he would have to say next. 'I've asked for some sort of a meal for us both—there's no one in the canteen for another half hour; we can go over the cases while we eat—it will save time in the morning.'

She was sure she was too befuddled by sleep to discuss anything, but it didn't enter her head to protest. They said goodnight to Night Sister and the staff nurse, and Mr Grenfell added his thanks with his usual polished courtesy, then they went down to the floor below and along to the canteen, where Eugenia was astonished to find a table in a corner ready laid for them and someone waiting to bring them soup and then steak and kidney pie and great cups of coffee. They hardly spoke at first; the food was hot and they were hungry, but presently Mr Grenfell said:

'I'm sorry about your evening, Eugenia. I'll see Humphrey tomorrow morning and explain. You've seen him?'

She nodded her head. 'Yes, but I really didn't have time...'

'Quite. A busy evening.' He smiled at her so kindly that she asked: 'You were going out too?'

'Yes, but Miriam is accustomed to doing without me on occasion—there's always someone to take my place.' He spoke without bitterness. 'Now, this girl—what's her name? Maureen—fifteen, and luckily strong and healthy and with parents who will take the greatest care of her...'

Her went into details about what had been done, and Eugenia, despite her fatigue, listened carefully; he wasn't a man to repeat instructions needlessly. 'And that first case—a Miss Brent, isn't it? I think we may have to send her to a good convalescent home away from the city once she's fit to move, and Mrs Stone—by some miracle the sliver of steel I got out of her hadn't touched anything vital—you'll have to keep a sharp eye on her, though...'

It was after midnight when they got up to go, and the first of the night nurses were trickling in for their meal. Outside the canteen Mr Grenfell paused.

'Goodnight, Eugenia. Thank you for being my good right hand once again. I'll see you in the morning.'

She bade him a sleepy goodnight and made for the nurses' home. She hoped she had taken in all that he had told her; tomorrow when her head felt clear, she would go over it all.

She slept at once, and woke at her usual time. She was a little pale at breakfast, but the day before her was a challenge not to be ignored. She gave the bare outlines of her evening's work to her companions, received their sympathy in her turn because she had missed an evening at the theatre, and went along to her ward.

Mr Grenfell and Harry were both there. Eugenia paused on her way to the office to wish them good morning and ask if they needed anything.

'Everything is just as it should be,' said Mr Grenfell. 'You've got to take the report? Come here afterwards, if you would be so kind.'

The report took them longer than usual, but nothing untoward had happened. Eugenia sent the night staff off duty, made sure that Hatty and her own nurses knew what they had to get on with, and enquired if they had all had supper when they had gone off duty the previous evening. 'I'll see you get your overtime made up,' she promised, 'but you may have to wait a day or two until things settle down.'

No one minded about that; it had been, in a way, exciting even though they had been run off their feet. Besides, they liked her, and they had already heard via the grapevine that it had been well past midnight by the time she had gone to her own bed.

She went down the ward then, saying good morning to the patients as she went, looking unflustered and capable of dealing with any situation. Mr Grenfell and Harry were still with Miss Brent, conscious now but hardly feeling herself. But Mr Grenfell could assume a most reassuring bedside manner when necessary; she watched the patient reviving under his bland reassurance, and then gently removed her gown so that the dressings might be inspected. 'Very nice,' said Mr Grenfell. 'We'll have you up and about in no time, Miss Brent. My registrar'—he nodded towards Harry—'will be visiting the ward twice a day, as well as my house surgeons. They're fully informed about your case, so you can safely confide in them. And Sister Smith is here too for most of the day; she's a most experienced nurse and will make sure you have all the attention you require.'

It was quite a long fulsome speech, and Eugenia was surprised. It wasn't until they had taken a look at Mrs Stone and pronounced her comfortable and had gone back to the office to write up the charts that Mr Grenfell observed: 'Miss Brent is what's commonly known as highly strung—a revolting expression and quite inaccurate. However, she's quite capable of having hysterics, I believe—certainly she's going to be difficult. I would suggest moving her bed next to the door, Sister, but if you did so I fear she would at once imagine she was about to die.' He smiled at her and she saw then that he was tired to the bone, even though he was as immaculate as he always was. Not enough sleep, she thought. 'We'll move her on as soon as it's safe to do so. As for Mrs Stone, she'll do very well, and Maureen has picked up nicely. They'll be sending her up here in an hour or so—have you enough staff?'

'I shall want one more nurse to cover the afternoon. I'll see the Office.'

At the door he said: 'You slept, Sister?'

'Very well, thank you, sir.' Her eyes looked the question she didn't like to ask.

He smiled. 'Sometimes it's pleasant to stay awake when one's thoughts are happy ones.'

'And what on earth made him say that?' wondered Eugenia aloud as she gathered up charts and notes and plunged into her busy day.

The next three or four days were busy too, and although she glimpsed Humphrey and even had a few moments' talk with him, she wasn't happy about it. He had been pleasant enough. Yes, he had taken his mother in her place to the theatre and it had been a very good show, it had been a pity that she hadn't been free. He had added in the tolerant voice she had come to expect and mistrust: 'Of course I quite understand that you couldn't leave the ward, Eugenia, but I do feel you should learn to delgate your responsibilities.'

She answered him in a reasonable voice: 'But I do, Humphrey, but don't you see, this was an emergency—a question of as many pairs of hands as we could muster.'

He had smiled in a superior way. 'In that case, other hands would have done just as well, wouldn't they?'

'Whose?' she had asked bluntly. 'Where would I have conjured up nurses at a moment's notice?'

'Now you're exaggerating,' he told her with smiling forbearance.

Perhaps, she told herself afterwards, it would be a good idea if she and Humphrey didn't see each other for a day or two. She had a free evening; she would go home, somewhere where she could air her grievances, real and imaginary, and be sure of an audience.

They were pleased to see her, as they always were. She sat in the easy chair opposite her father with Plum on her knee, and told him all about it. The twins were there too, of course, ostensibly doing their homework while they listened to every word she said.

'Gerard told us you'd been worth your weight in gold,' observed Becky.

Eugenia turned her head to frown at her young sister. 'But when did you see him?'

'Oh—yesterday, was it? No, the day before. He brought another book for Father. He said he was sorry your evening with Humphrey had been spoilt.' Becky added: 'Can't Humphrey buy some more tickets for another evening?'

'Well, no. These tickets were complimentary.' Eugenia ignored the look the twins exchanged. 'Anyway, he took his mother instead of me, so they weren't wasted.'

The short companionable silence was broken by Becky. 'When are you and Humphrey going to get married?'

Eugenia looked at her sister speechlessly. After a moment she said lamely: 'Well, we're engaged . . .'

'You don't have to get married just because you're engaged—you can fall in love and get married,' Becky flicked her thumb and finger together, 'in a few days if you really want to.' She went on with horrid persistence: 'Did you and Humphrey fall in love at first sight?'

'Yes—no. I can't remember, it was so long ago.' Eugenia looked at Becky helplessly, her usual calm quite shattered. She couldn't for the life of her remember what she had felt when she had first seen Humphrey. She said finally: 'You—you get to know each other . . .'

'I'd rather fall in love first,' declared Becky. 'I mean really in love, so that you didn't mind if he was cross-eyed or had a moustache. There's heaps of time to get to know him once you're married.'

Mr Smith coughed gently. 'I'd rather you married a young man who was clean-shaven and with normal eyesight,' he suggested gently—a remark which relieved the tension, so that they were all laughing again.

All the same, Eugenia couldn't get Becky's words out of her head. Surely, if she really loved Humphrey, she would remember how she had felt at the beginning? And surely if she loved him enough to marry him, she would be able to cope with his mother and not mind one scrap? She went to bed at last, telling herself she was tired and couldn't think straight. All the same, it took her a long time to get to sleep.

CHAPTER SEVEN

It was Mr Grenfell's round in the morning, a little protracted because he made examinations of the three emergencies. 'Very satisfactory,' he observed, as she poured coffee in the office afterwards. 'Sister, I shall be away next week. Harry will deal with the cases which have been booked and take over the rounds. There are a couple of pneumonectomies for the week after—both chesty.' He turned to Harry. 'Get them going with the physiotherapist, will you?'

They discussed the patients for a short time, and when he got up to go, Mr Grenfell bade Eugenia a rather aloof goodbye before walking back through the ward with Harry hard on his heels, the house surgeon trailing behind and Eugenia at his side. At the door he paused again. 'I'm going to the Algarve,' he told her, and added silkily: 'Miriam has always wanted to visit it—one of the few places she hasn't been to.'

'I hope you enjoy your holiday, sir.'

He stared down at her. Presently he nodded and went away.

The week crawled by. For once the ward wasn't unduly busy and Eugenia got off duty on time. True to her resolve, she managed to avoid Humphrey for the greater part of it, although on the Saturday she committed herself to spending the evening with him.

The weather was splendid for early May and she got into the blue suit and a silk blouse, wondering where they would go. It was quite true—that old adage about absence making the heart grow fonder; it would be lovely to spend an evening together. The cinema, she wondered, or a meal out in some modest restaurant? She found a bag to match the new shoes, gave a final glance in the looking glass, and went out to the car park where the residents' cars were parked. To reach it she had to pass the area set aside for the consultants' cars. The end square was empty, the Bentley wasn't there. She hadn't expected it to be, but suddenly she wished very much to be in the Algarve again. With hindsight, she saw that it had been a very happy time, even though she had been run off her feet. And yet, she recalled, she hadn't been able to wait to get back to London and Humphrey. There was no time to puzzle that one out; Humphrey was sitting in the car, sounding his horn in impatient little blasts.

Eugenia got in beside him and saw with relief that he looked pleased to see her. So he had got over his ill-humour; bent on keeping it that way, she enquired after his week.

'Extremely busy; I seem to be taking on more and more work.' He spoke importantly and she asked:

'Oh, why is that?'

'There's a houseman off sick. Someone has to do the routine work—I have to cope with that as well as my own.'

He didn't ask her about her own week and after a moment she asked cheerfully: 'Where are we going? It's nice to have a whole special evening to ourselves.'

Humphrey started the car. 'As a matter of fact, Mother has some of the family staying with her—cousins and my aunt and uncle. You've not met them yet—I thought that it would be a good opportunity to get to know them.'

She said uncertainly: 'But, Humphrey, we haven't seen each other all week . . .'

'My dear girl, we're fortunately in a position to take our engagement at a sober pace so that we don't have to fall into the depths of despair if we're unable to see each other every day, or even every other day.' He laughed a little and patted her knee. 'You really must grow up, Eugenia.'

A not very satisfactory answer, but one which she had to be content with.

They were welcomed effusively by Mrs Parsons, and Eugenia was left for a moment while Humphrey greeted a mild-looking elderly man, a thin, severe-looking woman who she suspected was his wife, and two young women in their thirties. They were both plain, although they need not have been if they had changed their hair-styles and done something to their faces. They stared at Eugenia until Humphrey introduced them all—Uncle Tom, Aunt Iris and Vera and Claudia. They shook hands, and Mrs Parsons cried in her girlish fashion: 'This is my dear little daughter-in-law-to-be—a nurse, you know, at St Clare's—so nice that she can take an interest in Humphrey's work.'

Eugenia pinned a smile to her face. Mrs Parsons had managed to make her sound inferior to everyone in the room. To call her little was stupid for a start, she loomed several inches over Mrs Parsons, and she was a Ward Sister, way past the elementary chores Mrs Parson's words had conjured up.

And Humphrey could have said something, but he merely stood there smiling; she would have something to say to him later on.

In the meanwhile there was a glass of sherry to drink while she made a slow-moving conversation with one of the cousins, and then supper, sitting between Uncle Tom and the other cousin—an elaborate meal, with Mrs Parsons explaining in a die-away voice just how long it had taken her to shop for each item they ate, and the unsparing efforts made to offer some of her most cherished recipes to her guests.

They drank their coffee in the drawing room—a dreadful beverage, tepid and not entirely free from grounds—and made more polite conversation. The evening was almost over when Eugenia realised that she hadn't spoken to Humphrey at all. Her relief was great when he said importantly that he was on call at midnight and that they would have to leave. 'I have to be ready for any emergency,' he added impressively. 'You're ready, Eugenia?'

More than ready. She went the round of the Parsons family, aware of their indifference to her. Perhaps they would get to like her when they knew her better—once she and Humphrey were married. She kissed Mrs Parsons dutifully and got into the car beside Humphrey, listening to her last-minute instructions about clean socks and making sure to eat enough and get all the sleep possible.

He got into the car, laughing a little. 'I hope you'll look after me as well as Mother does,' she heard him say lightly.

'That won't terribly matter if she's living with us,' said Eugenia tartly, a remark which called forth nothing but a pained silence until they reached the hospital. As they got out of the car, he said: 'You're very irritable, Eugenia—perhaps you need a holiday. Couldn't you arrange one?'

He spoke with a forbearance which set her teeth on edge, and certainly did nothing to improve her temper. They were standing beside the car, she to go round to the front entrance, and he to go through the small side door which gave on to the residents' quarters. 'I was looking forward to our evening,' she said. 'Do you know, you didn't speak to me the whole time?'

He smiled at her. 'I haven't seen my cousins for some time—I can see you whenever I like, within reason.'

Which reply made Eugenia's beautiful eyes glitter with unusual temper. She bit back words she longed to utter, although they almost choked her. She turned on her heel and walked away without a backward glance, round the side of the building and in through the entrance.

Mr Grenfell was standing just inside the door, gazing at nothing just above her head. He lowered his gaze and allowed a look of surprise to show on his handsome face. 'Ah, Eugenia—a pleasant evening, I hope?' He looked at the thin gold watch on his wrist. 'But rather early, isn't it?'

She said through her teeth, not caring any more: 'Humphrey is on call at midnight.'

'But it's barely half past nine.' His heavy lids dropped even lower. 'Have you been having words again?'

'Words? Words?' she glared at him. 'He's not spoken to me all the evening—all those beastly cousins . . .' Her bosom heaved with strong emotion, and Mr Grenfell took her arm and turned her round and walked her out of the hospital again. 'You need to get this off your chest,' he observed in a positively fatherly voice. 'We'll go somewhere and have a cup of coffee.'

There was a café of sorts across the street, which while lacking the luxurious look of its better class fellows, served simple meals, well cooked, and excellent coffee and tea. Mr Grenfell urged her gently through the door and sat her down at one of the plastic-covered tables. The place was fairly full and rang with cheerful voices all talking at once.

'Ideal,' murmured Mr Grenfell. 'Have you had a meal?'

'I had supper at Humphrey's mother's house.' She tried to sound casual about it, but her voice was wobbly with temper still.

'Just so. How about a pot of tea, buttered teacakes and jam? I like jam.'

Eugenia said wistfully, temper for the moment forgotten: 'I used to make jam with Mother. We had a big garden—redcurrants and plums and gooseberries and strawberries and raspberries.'

'The kind of garden children should grow up in,' said Mr Grenfell softly. 'I did.'

'Yes. Is there a kitchen garden at your house?'

'A small one, but we had—still have—a cottage in the country.' He paused to give the order to the restaurant's proprietor. 'Now, Eugenia, suppose you tell me all about it, you'll feel better if you do—regard me as *in loco parentis* if you wish.'

'You're not that old,' she declared, and then: 'Are you?'

'Going steadily downhill towards forty,' he observed placidly. 'I quite thought that you'd made it up with Humphrey.'

'Well, yes—at least, I kept away from him for almost a week, and when he said we'd go out this evening I thought it would be to a restaurant or the flicks—just us, you know, but instead of that we went to his mother's and there were these cousins and an uncle and aunt . . .! If I'd known perhaps I wouldn't have minded so much.' She paused while the tea and the teacakes were put on the table. 'It's just that I was very disappointed.'

Mr Grenfell offered her a teacake, butter and jam, and observed comfortably: 'The course of true love never did run smooth, Eugenia.'

She poured their tea and handed him the cup and saucer. 'Have I been silly?' she wanted to know.

'Humphrey said I was irritable and that a holiday might make me feel better.'

'Do you want a holiday?'

She thought about it, sinking her strong white teeth into the buttery teacake. 'No, I don't think I do. What good would it be anyway? You see, if I'm busy I don't have much time to think . . .'

Mr Grenfell gave her a bright glance from under his lids. 'In that case follow your own inclinations. Are you tired?'

She shook her head. 'But I daresay I shall be by the time I get back. It was kind of you . . . I'm grateful. It was nice to have someone to talk to.'

'I'm not tired either.' He had ignored her floundering thanks. 'I feel the need of movement—fresh air. Would you care to come for a drive? The car's at St Clare's. It's a splendid night and not cold, and I'll have you back by midnight?'

It was ten o'clock already. 'Where should we go?' she asked.

'Oh, a short run, into Essex—the rural Essex.'

Prudence took over briefly. 'I don't really think——' she began, and stopped when she saw that he was amused, so that prudence had no chance. 'I'd like that,' she said.

The streets were fairly quiet by now. They went back and got into the Bentley and drove down the Mile End Road, through Manor Park and the East End streets to Romford where he turned off to pick up the road to Chipping Ongar and then on to Great Bardfield. They were on minor roads now, with almost no traffic, and presently Eugenia asked: 'Do you know this road very well?'

'Yes. We're almost at the cottage where I spend what time I can spare.'

They had reached Great Bardfield, and now he turned the car into a country road. 'Little Bardfield,' he told her. 'The cottage is just before the village.' He added: 'The lilac should be out.'

He stopped the car about a mile further on and got out and opened the door for her. It was a lovely night with a moon shining from a starry sky. Eugenia could see the cottage clearly. It wasn't really a cottage, but a fair-sized thatched house, surrounded by a stone and brick wall and screened by trees. Its windows were latticed and those upstairs peeped from heavy thatched eyebrows.

They crossed the road and stood at the gate, looking at it.

'Nice?' asked Mr Grenfell.

'Lovely! How can you bear not to live here?' She added hastily: 'Though your house in Chelsea is lovely too.'

'I spend quite a lot of time here.' He was leaning on the gate beside her. 'Pringle and Mrs Pringle come with me, and the animals, of course, and there's a woman in the village who comes in regularly to see that everything is as it should be. Can you smell the lilac?'

'Yes.' She sniffed appreciatively. 'Lilac trees here and a bluebell wood.'

He opened the gate. 'Stay there if you like.' He had gone down the path before she could answer him, to reappear a few minutes later. 'The bluebells are over for this year, but perhaps this will do instead,' he said, and put an armful of lilac into her arms. 'Now we'd better get back.'

Eugenia got back into the car and he put the lilac on the back seat, got in beside her and started the car. Eugenia had quite forgotten that she had been filled with rage only a few hours before, and she felt content and a little sleepy. 'This is heavenly, Mr Grenfell,' she said gratefully.

'Off and on I'm Gerard—I hope it's an on evening.'

She laughed a little. 'All right, Gerard, only I must remember to call you Mr Grenfell at the hospital.'

'You sound sleepy! Close your eyes.'

'It's not very sociable,' she objected.

'We're past that stage,' he said quietly, and she sat pondering that as they drove back down the narrow road, through Great Bardfield again and on towards London. Long before they reached its outskirts she had closed her eyes and slept.

She woke as he turned into the hospital entrance. 'What you must think of me!' she began contritely. 'I'm sorry—what a bore for you . . .'

'No. Driving with someone sleeping peacefully beside one is very soothing.' He gave her an intent look. 'Do you feel better?'

'Oh, yes—yes, I do, Gerard. Somehow you've blown all the bogies away. I've been very silly, and I'll tell Humphrey so when I see him.'

He opened her door and she got out and waited while he got the lilac.

'Thank you for a lovely evening—and these.' She touched the flowers with a gentle finger. She stared up at him. 'I think you're very wise.'

'Not particularly, but I have unbounded patience. You might remember that, Eugenia. Goodnight!'

She woke in the night, aware of the sweet smell of the lilac she had put in her washbasin. When she woke in the morning she couldn't remember what she had thought then, only that she had felt very happy. The feeling persisted all day, through the routine of the ward and Harry's visits and dealing with the relatives who came pouring in after dinner. It was Hatty's weekend, and she had chosen to take an hour or two off in the morning, because someone had to be available to talk to anyone who wanted to know how their wives and mothers and daughters were getting on.

There had been no sign of Humphrey, but she hadn't expected to see him. Even if they had parted on the best of terms he would be busy on the medical side if he was on call and probably far too tired to spend half an hour together once they were off duty. It didn't seem right, somehow, she mused, pausing, her pen positioned over the laundry list. Surely when you were in love you wanted to spend every second with each other, even if you were too tired to talk? Or was that just romantic nonsense?

She went back to her list, the happiness she had felt all day oozing away. She must, she decided, have a talk with Humphrey. The trouble was that they didn't have enough time together to talk, discuss things, get their future settled for once and for all.

It was the middle of the week before she had the chance to spend an hour or two with him. Monday had been quiet, admitting patients, discharging others, and on Tuesday Mr Grenfell had done his round, remotely polite, treating her with his usual courtesy but displaying no interest in her as a person. She found it hard to believe, as she accompanied him from bed to bed, that this was the man who had driven her through the moonlight and filled her arms with lilac. She matched his manner with her own, coolly friendly and professional, so that Hatty, who had once or twice lately thought that they were becoming friends at last, decided she had made a mistake. It quite upset her, especially as the new house surgeon had asked her out, and being a little in love herself, she wanted everyone else to be as happy as she was.

Eugenia was free on Wednesday evening and so was Humphrey. She had waited all day for him to phone and arrange to meet her, but by five o'clock she realised she would have to be the first to offer the olive branch. He was knee-deep in forms and notes, he told her when she rang, but he would meet her at the hospital entrance at half past seven. He had sounded a little terse, but she put that down to the amount of work he had to do. They could walk across the road to the café, have a meal and talk; it wouldn't be busy at that hour and they would be able to sit there for as long as they liked.

It was a bright evening, still cool, but the sky was blue, already tinged with a splendid sunset. Eugenia showered and changed without haste, filled in time by phoning home, and then went down to the entrance.

Humphrey wasn't there. She passed the time of day with the porter on duty and then leant against his cubbyhole reading the evening paper he had lent her.

There were people coming and going all the time, but she didn't look up. Humphrey would come from the hospital, through one of the corridors at the back of the entrance hall. But she couldn't help but recognise the firm tread of Mr Grenfell's large well-shod feet as he came through the doors.

'That's a funny way to spend the evening,' he commented, coming to a halt by her.

'Waiting for Humphrey,' she explained. 'I daresay he's been held up.'

Mr Grenfell stood looking down at her. Doctor Parsons had been off duty for at least an hour; he'd been in the Common Room when he had gone there himself to speak to Harry. He didn't mention the fact, but said smoothly: 'Well, enjoy your evening together.' He turned away and then retraced his steps. 'There's a case coming in tomorrow morning—I've just been to look at her. She'll be a lobectomy, I fancy. There's a bed?'

'Oh, yes. Thanks for letting me know.' She smiled at him, unaware that Humphrey had just entered the hall and was coming slowly towards them. But Mr Grenfell must have seen him, because he swung round to meet him.

'Evening, Parsons. Did you get hung up on something at the last minute?' He nodded affably. 'Enjoy yourselves.'

He went on his way, and Humphrey said: 'What was he saying to you?' His voice held a faint sneer. 'Coaxing you to take another trip?'

Eugenia said slowly: 'No, nothing like that—only that there's an unexpected case coming in in the morning. Where shall we go?'

'I should have liked to have visited Mother, but since you're always complaining that we're never alone, we'd better go and have a meal, I suppose.'

'That would be nice. We can talk . . .'

He took her arm and they started to cross the forecourt. 'Ah yes—I really must tell you about that leukaemia case on Men's Medical . . .'

That hadn't been quite what she had meant, but she listened with real interest, made intelligent comments, and curbed her desire to talk about themselves. She was rewarded by her forbearance, for presently, when they were seated at a corner table in the same café she and Mr Grenfell had visited, Humphrey put down the menu and asked smilingly: 'Well, what have you been doing with yourself? Not too busy?' His question was casual. 'And quite recovered from your little outburst, I hope?'

'Yes. I'm sorry about that, although I meant every word of it . . .' She saw his quick frown, but before he could say anything the proprietor was at the table waiting to know what they would like. Eugenia chose beans on toast and an egg and a pot of tea and waited while Humphrey decided between soup of the day and fishcakes or bacon and eggs. He ordered coffee for himself, pointing out that she drank too much tea as it was.

'I missed tea today,' she told him cheerfully. 'One of my ladies took a nasty turn . . .' She paused, because there was a faint impatience on his face, but only for a moment. 'Humphrey, do you want me to go on working after we're married?'

'Now, why on earth do you want to bring that up?' He gave her a light tolerant smile. 'I never knew such a girl! Time enough to decide that once we've settled on a date.'

The tea came and she poured herself a cup. 'Let's settle the date now?' she suggested.

His smile was still tolerant. 'Darling, what's come over you? I was doing some sums a day or so ago, and if we save hard, we should be able to get married in eighteen months' time; let's wait until then before making any more plans.'

She said a little desperately. 'Yes, but don't you feel that we're wasting time—losing something? We could find a small flat and I'd go on working and we could still save . . .'

'We've gone over this before, Eugenia, and you know my views. I want security, my own home, a future free from uncertainties. Maybe we're waiting a little longer than most couples before we get married, but we'll have no worries about mortgages or hire-purchase.'

'Won't we—everything—be a little stale by then?' she asked.

'I can't imagine why you should say that. Security is important above all else, especially in married life.'

'What about love?' Eugenia drew a deep breath and plunged. 'Humphrey, why don't we go away for a weekend together? I mean on our own—stay somewhere quiet. It might ... that is, we might feel like we did when we first met.'

He took a mouthful of bacon with deliberation. 'I said last week that you needed a holiday, my dear. I'll repeat that; you're overwrought and exhausted for some reason and don't realise what you're saying. I don't agree with pre-marital relationships. I'm glad Mother didn't hear you say that, she would have been profoundly shocked!'

'I'm a bit shocked myself,' said Eugenia. 'Only I— thought that perhaps it might help—sort of stir things up a bit.' She stopped again, because he was looking vexed. 'You don't like the idea?'

'Certainly not, and I should be glad if you don't bring up the subject again. If you've finished, how about a brisk walk? Probably you don't get sufficient exercise.'

She didn't see him for a couple of days after that, which was perhaps just as well, because she felt quite at outs with him. When they had first become engaged, saving for a home had been fun, but it had never entered her head that the saving would have to go on for so long. It seemed to her that their love for each other was being swamped by Humphrey's precise calculations, just as it seemed that the list of things which were quite indispensable to their marriage grew longer and longer each month.

She went home one evening, but somehow she was unable to talk about it. It had gone too deep, she realised; now it was something she and Humphrey must work out for themselves. If only she could make him see!

She wasn't sleeping very well and she had lost her appetite, although her work didn't suffer. All the same, when she met Mr Grenfell on the way to X-ray one morning he stopped in front of her and asked: 'What's wrong? No, don't tell me, I'll guess. Humphrey's set his sights on a dishwashing machine and put the wedding off for another couple of months?'

There was no sneer in his voice, he had meant it as such a joke, and Eugenia tried to answer him in the same spirit. 'Something like that. I'm too impatient. I think he's right, I need a holiday. Perhaps I'll take one.'

'I wish you would, and solve a problem for me. Mrs Pringle has had a severe attack of bronchitis. I want her to have a week at the cottage, but she won't go on her own, naturally enough, and Pringle says he can't leave the house to the daily maids. If you'd go with her ...' he paused and smiled at her. 'You'd make three people happy; Mrs Pringle, Pringle and me. You'd not have anything to do, just see that she takes her pills and takes life easily.'

'You're joking,' said Eugenia, and was answered by his grave:

'No, I'm not. Why should I do that? You mentioned that you might take a holiday and it seemed like a gift from heaven. Take it or leave it.'

She told herself afterwards that she had never intended to agree. She had done so on the spur of the moment, some small demon inside her had prompted her. She spent the rest of the day wondering what excuse she could make so that she could refuse to take up his offer, and decided that she wouldn't make one, only tell him that she hadn't meant to say yes and that she really didn't want a holiday after all.

Only she had no opportunity to do so. True, he did a round the next day, but that was hardly the time or the place in which to discuss the matter with him. If he had just so much as mentioned the matter it would have made it easier, but he was more remote than usual; perfectly polite, even friendly in an impersonal way, but he gave her no chance to say a word other than those concerning strictly surgical matters. Eugenia saw him go with a smouldering eye and presently went off duty, to bump into Humphrey coming from the medical wing. She stopped in front of him, relieved that here was someone in whom she could confide. 'Humphrey, did you mean it, the other evening when you said that I needed a holiday?'

He changed a pile of case notes from one arm to the other. 'Yes, yes, of course I did, Eugenia, but don't stop me now; I'm extremely busy. I'm glad you're taking my advice for once.' He took a step away from her. 'I'm late as it is . . .'

She swivelled on her heels and watched him stride away; handsome, undoubtedly clever, and quite frighteningly and suddenly a stranger who didn't want to be bothered with her small worries. 'I'll go, then,' she declared out loud so that one of the porters, passing her, turned round and asked: 'Did you say something, Sister?'

'No, Blake—just thought something out loud.'

Next morning she went to the Office and arranged for her week's leave. If Mr Grenfell's suggestion hadn't been a genuine one, it really didn't matter; she could always spend the week at home. But it was genuine all right; back in her office writing up the surgical supplies for the next day, she lifted the receiver when the phone rang and heard his voice.

'Ah, Eugenia. You have your holiday booked?' He had asked the question, but she had the feeling that he already knew the answer. All the same, she told him yes.

'Good, I'll collect you about nine o'clock on Saturday—it is your weekend, isn't it? I'll have Mrs Pringle with me. Do you want to call in on your family on the way?'

'No, thanks, I've got an evening off tomorrow, so I'll go home then.' There was a small silence, then she said stiffly: 'I saw Humphrey. I asked him if he thought it a good idea if I took a week off and he said yes.'

Mr Grenfell sounded very smooth. 'Ah, yes. There's no reason why he shouldn't visit you while you're at the cottage.'

She said reluctantly: 'He doesn't know I'm going there.' And when he didn't answer: 'I'll tell him before I go.'

'Naturally.' He sounded amused. 'Nine o'clock on Saturday, then.'

Eugenia went home the next evening and told her father that she would be away for a week. 'Mr Grenfell's housekeeper's been ill and he asked if I'd mind spending a week with her. It'll make a nice change.' There was a hint of defiance in her voice.

'What a splendid idea, Eugenia. A week in the country will do you a world of good. What does Humphrey say about it?'

'I haven't told him yet—I was going to, but he couldn't stop to listen. But I'll make a point of seeing him before Saturday. He—he told me I needed a holiday anyway.'

'In that case he should be delighted.'

She wasn't so sure about that, but all the same, she intended telling him. She was off duty on Friday evening, and perhaps they could go out for an hour and she would tell him then.

Humphrey was free after six, so he told her when she phoned him. He would meet her in the car park at half past the hour. He didn't say more; he didn't like her phoning him at his flat, still less in the ward—something she never did unless it was urgent. She wasn't late off duty, she showered and changed into a jersey dress and found a cardigan to go with it; it was a pleasant enough evening and she supposed they would drive out of town and have a meal. They hadn't done that for a long time, and surely it was something they could afford once in a while.

One of the housemen was talking to Humphrey as she reached his car, so she merely said, 'Hullo', and smiled as she got in, waiting patiently until they had finished their conversation.

Humphrey was in a good mood, condescending about young newly qualified doctors. 'Very uncertain of himself,' he observed, taking the car out of the forecourt and into the street.

'Well, I suppose we all are, when we start something new,' said Eugenia mildly. 'Where are we going?'

'Mother phoned—she's having trouble with her tax returns; it seems a good chance to sort them out for her. She'll give us supper.'

'I thought we were going to have an evening together—it seems a long time . . .'

'Yes, well, we'll go out next week. I've got an evening on Wednesday. I can't leave Mother to worry herself sick . . .'

'Couldn't she get help? An accountant or the bank?'

'When I can see to it for nothing?' He laughed gently. 'Darling, you're sometimes quite lacking in common sense!'

It didn't seem the right moment to mention her holiday.

It was on the way back to the hospital that she at last managed to tell him; the evening had been a dead loss, with Humphrey poring over endless forms and Mrs Parsons fluttering to and fro with sandwiches and unspeakable coffee. 'I do remember saying that I'd give you supper,' she explained in her little-girl voice, 'but I've been so worried about these silly taxes that I couldn't bring myself to cook.' She added: 'It would have been nice if we could have gone out for a meal . . .'

'The sandwiches are very nice, Mrs Parsons,' said Eugenia. 'Humphrey and I are quite used to scratch meals.'

Not very happily put, she had realised, catching Mrs Parsons' incensed eye. Now, with St Clare's red bricks in sight, she said: 'I'm going away for a week tomorrow.'

'Ah, you took my advice.' Humphrey sounded smug. 'I knew you would!'

'No, I didn't take your advice. Mr Grenfell's housekeeper has been ill and I'm going to spend a week in the country with her at Mr Grenfell's cottage.'

She had often wondered what a pregnant silence was. She knew now. Humphrey turned the car into the forecourt, drove round to the car park and stopped. Only then did he turn round to look at her. 'Have you taken leave of your senses?' he demanded. It struck her that he didn't sound annoyed, only tolerantly amused. 'Of course you'll do no such thing,' he went on in the same tolerant way. 'I've never heard of anything so silly!'

'It's not silly. You said I ought to take a holiday—well, Mrs Pringle needs to go away for a week and doesn't want to go alone. It'll be a nice change.'

'You've met Mrs Pringle?'

Perhaps it was best not to go into that. 'She's Mr Grenfell's housekeeper—I've just told you that. She's elderly—well housekeepers generally are, aren't they?

She's had bronchitis.' She added recklessly: 'Don't you think it sounds a good idea?'

Humphrey sighed a little dramatically. 'You have changed lately, Eugenia, but you must do as you wish. On several occasions in the last few weeks you've gone against my wishes. Perhaps a week away would be a good idea.'

'You could come and see me.' She tried not to sound wistful.

'That would be ridiculous—I don't know where the cottage is, but presumably it's outside London. And you'll only be gone for a week.'

'Yes. Humphrey, will you miss me?'

He laughed. 'In a week? After all, we don't see much of each other in that time, do we? Perhaps when you get back we'll have an evening together.'

'Oh, Humphrey, yes! Let's splash out and have dinner and dance . . .'

He laughed again. 'I think a walk in Regent's Park and a meal out would do very nicely, don't you? No point in wasting money.'

She said soberly: 'No, Humphrey. You don't mind me going?'

'My dear girl, you're a grown woman and can make up your own mind, besides I advised you to have a week off—you'll be able to pull yourself together.' He pushed open his door. 'Well, I'm off to bed: I was up half of last night.' He leaned across and kissed her cheek. 'I shall expect a calm, sensible girl next time we meet.'

Eugenia opened her door and got out. 'Yes, Humphrey.'

He locked the car and gave her a casual pat on a shoulder. 'I won't come round to the entrance—no point, is there?' He laughed goodhumouredly. 'A great strapping girl like you can take care of herself!'

Eugenia said: 'Yes, Humphrey,' again. If he would kiss her—just once—properly, or tell her that he loved her . . . She found herself willing him to do the one or the other, but he turned away, lifting a hand as he went. 'See you,' he said. She watched him go through the side door before walking slowly round to the entrance and going inside. A good thing Mr Grenfell wasn't there this time, or she would have flung herself at him and burst into a flood of tears.

CHAPTER EIGHT

EUGENIA didn't sleep all that much. She lay in bed making excuses for Humphrey, telling herself she had been behaving foolishly and selfishly, that he had every reason to be annoyed. The trouble was, she couldn't pinpoint the exact trouble. Mrs Parsons was a stumbling block, of course, and Humphrey's increasing urge to save money at the expense of their happiness. For she had to admit, she wasn't happy. Being engaged should be delightful—there was no need to fling money around, but neither was there any need to scrape and screw for a future which was fast becoming unattractive. She dozed off towards morning and woke with a headache, far too early. She got up and made herself some tea, then packed a weekend case with slacks and shirts and a dress—she would not need much at the cottage anyway.

She made more tea, ate some biscuits, put on the blue suit and went down to the forecourt. Mr Grenfell had said nine o'clock, and if he was as punctual in his private life as he was on the ward, then she mustn't keep him waiting.

He was there, with Mrs Pringle in the back, looking under the weather but smiling cheerfully as Eugenia reached them. Mrs Pringle and Mr Grenfell wished her good morning, and he opened the door and ushered her in beside his housekeeper. She had expected to sit beside him and she gave him a quick, surprised glance as she settled herself. He met it with a small smile which told her nothing and got back in and drove off, lifting a casual hand in salute to the handful of people who had been watching them, hopeful of adding some titbit of gossip to the hospital grapevine.

Mrs Pringle, delighted to have someone to talk to, chatted happily for the entire journey. She still had a nasty cough, but that didn't deter her, and Eugenia, always a good listener, was a willing audience. Mr Grenfell said nothing at all. Indeed, she wondered once or twice if he had forgotten that he had passengers in the back of the car.

The cottage looked just as delightful in the May sunshine as it had in moonlight, but obviously Mr Grenfell wasn't feeling sentimental. He brushed past the lilac trees as though they weren't there, deposited their bags in the hall, introduced Eugenia to the middle-aged woman who had come from the village to open the house for them, drank a hasty cup of coffee and drove away again, declaring that he had an appointment for two o'clock. Not one word did he say about fetching them back again the following week; presumably he had already said something to Mrs Pringle about that. Eugenia wished him a calm goodbye and went indoors, resisting a strong desire to watch the Bentley until it was out of sight; despite Mrs Pringle's cheerful presence, she felt suddenly lonely.

Mrs Cobb, coming in from the kitchen as they went indoors again, beamed at them both. 'I'm sure it's proper nice to have someone here; haven't seen Mr Grenfell for dear knows how long. O' course, his fiancée don't like this place—too quiet. I suppose that's why he doesn't come, only on his own, like, for an hour or two.' She went on, hardly pausing for breath: 'There's a nice shepherd's pie in the oven and one of my custard tarts—will half an hour suit you?'

'You sit here,' suggested Eugenia to Mrs Pringle. 'I'll

unpack for us both, there's no need for you to go upstairs.'

'Well, that's kind of you, Sister Smith. I'll sit in the kitchen while Mrs Cobb finishes off the cooking and have a chat.'

Eugenia went up the small staircase. Mrs Cobb had taken their cases up and she went slowly, looking around her. The hall was roomy and square, furnished with some nice old chests and a wall table with a bowl of flowers on it. The floor was tiled, but most of it was covered by a patterned rug; the same pattern covered the stairs and the landing, and she stopped there to look around her. The furnishings were exactly right for a cottage and there was no lack of comfort; she discovered that when she went into the room which was to be hers. A nice square room with an old-fashioned casement window hung with flowered chintz; there was a pale rug on the polished wood floor and the bed and tallboy and dressing table were of yew. There was a small bathroom too, equipped with pastel towels, a bowl of soaps and an assortment of jars which she promised herself she would examine at her leisure. She unpacked her few things and went along to Mrs Pringle's room across the landing—the counterpart of hers, its window overlooking the side of the garden.

Eugenia paused in her unpacking to lean her elbows on the sill and gaze around her. The garden was delightful, a glorious mixture of fruit trees, shrubs, a mown lawn there, the glimpse of a vegetable patch behind a screen of beech, and flower beds round and about, all of them stuffed with spring flowers in full bloom. 'What a waste,' declared Eugenia, to no one in particular, 'to have such a lovely corner to live in and almost never come to it.' Of course, she reflected, carefully folding Mrs Pringle's voluminous nighties into a drawer, if Miriam didn't like it . . .

They ate their lunch without hurry, and then, mindful of Mr Grenfell's words, Eugenia popped Mrs Pringle on to her bed for a nap and went downstairs to give Mrs Cobb a hand with the washing up.

'Well, miss, I must say it's kind of you,' said that lady. 'You a Sister and all and on holiday, so I hear. I'll put the tea all ready for you before I go home and there's everything ready for your supper in the fridge. I'll be here at half past eight in the morning; breakfast at nine o'clock, and no need for you to do anything—dear knows I have little to do most of the time. I thought a nice bit of fish for tomorrow?'

'That sounds nice,' agreed Eugenia, hanging up her tea-towel. 'Lunch was lovely.'

Mrs Cobb visibly glowed. 'There's a nice bit of fruit cake for your tea,' she said. 'Mr Grenfell, he always likes a fruit cake—home-made, of course.'

'Of course. The shepherd's pie was delicious, Mrs Cobb.'

When the good lady had gone, Eugenia went into the garden. It was very quiet; just the sounds of the country she had known all her life before they had moved to London, and it was warm in the sheltered corners. She found a garden seat tucked away in a sunny place and sat down, more content than she had been for ages. She hadn't felt like that for a long time. No, not so long; she had felt exactly the same in the little bluebell wood in Mr Grenfell's garden.

She went back into the cottage presently and got tea ready, and Mrs Pringle, nicely rested, joined her in the comfortable sitting room.

'It's very kind of you, my dear,' said Mrs Pringle for the tenth time, 'spending your holiday with an old woman when you could be gadding about in foreign parts, and you so very pretty too. I daresay you've got a young man?' Her eyes slid to Eugenia's left hand.

'Yes—I've been engaged for a year or two. I—we—hope to get married as soon as it's possible.'

Mrs Pringle looked at her quite severely. 'And that'll be never, miss, if I might say so without giving offence. There's always something crops up ... But there, I daresay it's different with you. Me and Pringle, we married on next to nothing, but we managed. We've a daughter, you know—got a good job as a nanny—trained, she is.' She picked up her knitting and began clicking needles furiously. 'There's a clever pair you've got for brother and sister, miss. I daresay they do well at school?'

The evening passed pleasantly and they went to bed early, and the days which followed were just as pleasant. Mrs Pringle recovered rapidly. There was little to do for her other than reminding her to take her pills, and Eugenia spent blissful hours in the garden or wandering down to the village for odds and ends. She had given Humphrey her phone number, but he didn't ring her; she told herself that he was busy, and after all, he knew where she was and that she would be away for only a week. And she had half expected to hear from Mr Grenfell—after all, it was his housekeeper who was recovering from bronchitis, wasn't it? But the telephone remained silent, and she told herself that it was heavenly not to have the thing ringing all day long as it did on the Ward.

There were books in the sitting room. She read voraciously when she wasn't listening to Mrs Pringle's gentle chatter, winding wool, or giving Mrs Cobb a hand around the place, and almost without knowing it, she lost her London pallor. After the first day or two she walked each day, and what with pottering in the garden and doing the odd bit of shopping, she was tired enough to sleep all night. But it was the right kind of tiredness, not the exhaustion of a long hard day on the Ward. By Saturday she looked a different girl, and felt different too; even Mrs Parsons no longer seemed the stumbling block to the future that she had imagined.

'I've put on three pounds,' she told Mrs Pringle, 'and Humphrey—my fiancé—says I'm too fat as it is.'

'You're just right as you are,' Mrs Pringle assured her. 'Don't you lose an ounce, miss. Nice pink cheeks you've got too. I declare you never looked prettier. As for me, I never felt so ready to get back. Pringle's a good man, but he misses things—men do, you know.'

It was Friday night before Eugenia asked: 'Do you know what time we're leaving tomorrow, Mrs Pringle? I've not heard . . .'

'Bless you, Mr Grenfell telephoned this morning while you were out. After lunch, he said, and will we be sure to have some of Mrs Cobb's cake for his tea.'

So Eugenia packed their bags after breakfast the next morning, did her face very carefully without knowing why, and went into the garden for a final prowl. Time enough to change out of her cotton sweater and elderly skirt when they had had lunch. There was a great deal of rhubarb down at the bottom, behind the potting shed, and Mrs Pringle had declared herself anxious to make rhubarb jam. Forgetful of her careful make-up, Eugenia set about pulling vast quantities of it and sat down happily to trim the stalks of their leaves. She was piling them neatly in the trug she had brought with her when a small sound behind her made her look up. Mr Grenfell was leaning against an apple tree, watching her.

She was scarcely aware of the surge of feeling as she caught sight of him. She brushed back a lock of hair with an earthy hand and said in a calm way: 'Good morning, Mr Grenfell.'

'Gerard.'

She smiled. 'Gerard.' She lopped off another leaf or two. 'I don't think Mrs Pringle expected you until this afternoon.'

'I found I could get away earlier.'

Eugenia picked up the trug and got to her feet. 'Do you want to leave earlier? I'll get the . . .'

He interrupted her impatiently. 'Good heavens, girl, I've only just got here, intent on a couple of hours' peace and quiet!'

'Oh. Well, in that case I've got time to pull some more rhubarb. Have you had a busy week?'

'Yes.' He sounded quite testy. 'I—we all missed you. Hatty is an excellent nurse, but of course being in the throes of first love, she's the smallest bit distraite.'

Eugenia sat up. 'Hatty—in love? How absolutely splendid! Not with that nice young houseman who's just joined your firm?'

'The very same.' Mr Grenfell left the tree and folded his bulk tidily beside her. 'Love at first sight, from the look of it.'

'Oh, how simply marvellous! Hatty's such a dear and just right for him. I shall do all I can to encourage them.'

Mr Grenfell closed his eyes. 'Has Humphrey been down to see you?'

Eugenia bent down and pulled a radish from the neat row in the bed at her feet. She dusted it off rather perfunctorily and popped it into her mouth.

'No,' she said between crunches.

'Telephoned?'

'Why do you ask such questions?' asked Eugenia tartly. 'I don't ask you questions.'

'Very wise of you, Eugenia. What's for lunch?'

She turned to look at him. His eyes were still closed; he looked remarkably handsome, but also very tired.

'Roast chicken, bread sauce, stuffing, baked potatoes, baby carrots, spring greens, and apple tart and cream for afters.' She added: 'Have you been up all night?'

He opened one eye. 'More or less.'

'You could have a nap before lunch, it's only just eleven o'clock.'

'Mrs Cobb's making coffee. Are you looking forward to coming back to St Clare's?'

'No, not in the least. I've loved every minute of being here—I can't thank you enough. Mrs Pringle's quite recovered—you've seen her?'

'Yes. My thanks for bearing her company—we're both grateful.' He turned his head to smile at Mrs Cobb, carrying a tray.

'There's two cups,' she pointed out unnecessarily. 'You could do with another cup, Miss Eugenia? All that rhubarb too! We'll have to have you back when the strawberries are ripe.'

'What a good idea.' Mr Grenfell gave her a bland look. 'Another week's holiday some time in June?'

He was joking, of course, but she chose to answer him seriously. 'No more holidays until September. I believe Humphrey wants to go to Torquay.'

'À trois?' asked Mr Grenfell gently.

'Well, yes! Mrs Parsons has a friend there who keeps a boarding house. I couldn't go last year because Becky was ill with 'flu, but this year I shall go.'

Mr Grenfell drank his coffee and said nothing, staring at his garden with an inscrutable expression.

'Torquay's a very nice place,' said Eugenia edgily.

'I have no doubt it is. Better than this, Eugenia?' His voice was very soft.

'Don't be absurd,' she said roundly. 'You can't compare this place with Torquay. This is heaven—like your bluebell wood.' She took his cup from him. 'You've had your coffee, now you can have a sleep.'

He opened his eyes wide and she was, as always, surprised at their vivid blue. 'You're very solicitous, presumably making sure I shall be able to put in a good day's work on Monday.'

She laughed then. 'Don't be ridiculous, only you look tired.'

'And old?'

'No, not in the least. You don't feel old, do you?'

He grinned and the tired lines disappeared. 'No, I feel like a man who has found something he's been searching for all his life and knows that he'll get it.'

Eugenia frowned, not at all sure what he was talking about. Miriam perhaps? But he'd known about her months ago, when they had got engaged. Something rare he intended to buy? An award of some sort? He did a great deal of lecturing in his own field, perhaps he was to receive some award. She said rather primly: 'That's nice for you. I'm going to take this rhubarb indoors. Mrs Cobb's got a basket I can borrow.'

He picked up the trug and carried it to the kitchen for her and then wandered off. Eugenia could hear him talking to Mrs Pringle in the sitting room. She went upstairs and did her face again, then changed into the blue suit and rearranged her hair after which she sat down by the window with a book. There was still an hour until lunch and she didn't want to intrude.

Lunch was a leisurely meal, with Mrs Cobb popping in and out, pressing them to eat more of everything and stopping to drink a glass of wine when she brought in the apple pie. And when they had finished, Mrs Pringle went for what she called her little lay-down, Mr

Grenfell stretched his length in an armchair in the sitting room and Eugenia slipped into the kitchen to give Mrs Cobb a hand. They were to leave directly after tea, but Mrs Cobb would go home when the kitchen was clean and tidy again, leaving Eugenia to make the tea and cut the cake. 'And just you leave the dishes,' she begged Eugenia. 'I'll be in on Monday to give the place a good do, it's little enough I have to keep me busy here.' She brightened. 'Though Mr Grenfell did say I could expect him some time in June, bringing someone with him, he said.'

Miriam, thought Eugenia, and why not? The cottage in June would be irresistible even to the most hardened of town-dwellers.

They left after tea. Eugenia, sitting beside Mrs Pringle on the back seat, watched Mr Grenfell turn the key in the door and wished with all her heart that she could live the whole of the week again. London and St Clare's didn't bear thinking about.

It gave her quite a nasty shock to realise that she hadn't thought about Humphrey. She felt so guilty that the moment she had been dropped off at the hospital she had darted to the porter's lodge and asked the man to ring Humphrey. She was suddenly so obsessed with the wish to see him that she had hardly listened to Mr Grenfell's brief thanks and Mrs Pringle's rather more protracted ones. If Humphrey was free on Sunday they could go out for the evening. She was on duty, but only until five o'clock.

The porter handed her the phone and Humphrey's voice, rather sharp, sounded in her ear. 'Eugenia—so you're back! I'm very busy . . .'

She said tartly: 'Yes, I'm back, and I feel a lot better, thank you. I'm off at five o'clock tomorrow—perhaps we could go out for an hour?'

'After seven o'clock—I shall be very tired, but we might have a drink, I suppose.'

Eugenia reminded herself that he might have had a gruelling week. 'That will be nice. I'll meet you at the entrance about seven-thirty.' She rang off before he could reply.

Her room, after the pastel-tinted comfort of the cottage bedroom, looked bleak. She put her case down and without unpacking it, went back again out of the hospital and caught a bus out to her home.

They were all there; her father deep in a book, the twins worrying away at their homework like two puppies at a bone. They greeted her with delight, bombarded her with questions, observed plaintively that they were famished, and made her a pot of tea. Eugenia drank it curled up in one of the easy chairs in the sitting room and feeling much better because their welcome had been so warm, then went into the kitchen, where she made omelettes, french fries, a magnificent salad and a great pot of coffee.

Sitting round the table presently, she answered their questions all over again, and when her father asked: 'Did Humphrey go to see you, my dear?' she was able to say lightly:

'He's been so busy—we're going out tomorrow evening.'

'Oh, yes. Good.' Her father sounded vague. 'You look much better for your week's rest, anyway.'

Hatty said the same thing when she saw her in the morning, and indeed she did feel better; relaxed and full of sunshine and fresh air and Mrs Cobb's good food. Only the shabby streets round St Clare's looked even shabbier, and there wasn't a tree in sight . . .

The ward was busy, but not too much so. She was occupied all day, catching up on the new patients, reading notes, checking charts, mapping out the off-duty for the next couple of weeks. The hours slid past, five o'clock came and Eugenia handed over to Hatty and left the ward.

That young lady, reflected Eugenia, had changed overnight, as it were, from a chrysalis into a butterfly. Her plain face had taken on a glow, she had done her hair in a most fetching way, and unless Eugenia was very much mistaken, its mousiness had been discreetly tinted. Young love, mused Eugenia, feeling as old as Methuselah's wife.

It was a warm evening. Eugenia, intent on pleasing Humphrey, got into a jersey dress she had had for two years, found a cardigan to go with it, and went down to meet him.

She had to admit, a few hours later as she got ready for bed, that the evening hadn't been entirely successful. Humphrey had been edgy, ready to pick a quarrel if she but gave him the chance, so that she had to mind every word she said. He didn't want to hear about the cottage, or what she had done with her days; he was full of the inadequacies of the newest medical houseman, the problematic symptoms of a patient who had been admitted that day, and the annoying fact that the building society in which he had money had lowered its interest rates.

Eugenia had listened, at first with sympathy and then with a guilty feeling of boredom. She longed to tell him about the garden at the cottage, the lovely early morning freshness of the country, the long lazy afternoons ... but each time she tried, he swept her words away. 'Oh yes, I'm sure you had a lovely time, Eugenia. I only hope it's done you some good; you've been getting very unsettled—Mother noticed it too.' He had frowned a little. 'She needs a holiday,' he added. 'A pity Mr Grenfell doesn't extend his generosity to the elderly and the hard-working.'

Such an unfair remark that Eugenia hadn't been able to think of anything to say. Perhaps it was a good thing, she decided, getting into bed, that she wouldn't see Humphrey for a couple of days.

Monday was uneventful, so that she had time to catch up on her paperwork, familiarise herself with the newer patients, and skim through their notes. Mr Grenfell would be doing his round on the following morning and whether she had been away or not, he would expect her to know the answers to his questions.

It was a good thing she had done her homework, for he kept her on her toes for the entire round, remote and courteous and waiting politely while she sought for the right answers. And drinking coffee presently in her office, he had discussed his patients, made a few remarks about the weather, thanked her gravely at the ward door, and walked away without another word.

It wouldn't have hurt him to have said something—anything about her week's holiday. After all, she had spent it as his guest at the cottage, hadn't she? She gulped down the rest of her cooling coffee and bent her mind to the task of arranging the duty list so that Hatty could spend her days off with her admirer.

She had seen Humphrey for a few minutes that evening; he had a weekend, and so had she at the end of the following week. Without asking her how she felt about it, he told her that they would spend it with his mother.

There was no reason why the prospect should depress her so much. True, she never enjoyed being with Mrs Parsons, but until now she had accepted her as part of the future. She felt vaguely unhappy and slept so badly that she had a headache when she got up.

There were cases for Theatre after breakfast and she was kept busy. Indeed, going to her dinner was out of the question, so she had a pot of tea in the office, ate the rest of the biscuits from her store hoarded for coffee on round days, and went back into the ward. It was almost teatime before she felt satisfied with her patients, and Harry had been and gone for the last time. She supposed Mr Grenfell would come—he always did after he had been operating, but that wouldn't stop her going to tea. Half an hour off the ward would be bliss.

She was going out of her office door when he appeared, pushed her gently back inside and closed the door behind him.

Eugenia heaved a soundless sigh. 'You would like to see the operation cases, sir?'

'I have on my way here.' His voice was as remote as it had been on the round, and Eugenia wondered fleetingly if she had annoyed him in some way.

He looked over her head. 'Sister Smith, I should like you to accompany me at the end of this week. I have a consultation in Heidelberg—I shall probably operate.'

She thought of Humphrey and the weekend with his mother. 'Well, sir—I had arranged with Humphrey . . .'

He sounded testy. 'Your work is surely more important than a date with Parsons?' He suddenly glared down at her. 'It isn't as though either of you is in the throes of first love.'

Eugenia's magnificent bosom swelled under his appreciative eye. 'I've never heard . . .' she began, and caught his eye. He was amused, laughing at her behind that bland face. In a voice she strove to keep calm she began again. 'You're inconsiderate, Mr Grenfell,' and then, her feelings getting the better of her: 'And what might you know about young love?'

She stared up at him, appalled at what she had just said. What on earth had come over her?

His expression hadn't altered. 'I've outgrown that stage, but I suspect that love at any age can be just as intense; indeed, I don't suspect, I'm certain of it.'

'Oh, are you?' faltered Eugenia, feeling mean. He would be away from his Miriam, vain skinny creature that she was, still he must love her. And wasn't that a pity, what a waste ... Eugenia caught her breath on a sudden thought, bewildered and excited and sad. She wanted him for herself; all this time she had known it deep down inside her and never admitted it. Miriam would be the worst possible wife for him; what he needed was a woman who would put up with his absorption in his work, look after him when he was under the weather, wait up for him when he got home late, see what he needed and that his home was run smoothly, and above all, love him to distraction—just as she most surely did. And now, sadly, he would marry Miriam and she, she supposed, would marry Humphrey and four people would be unhappy for the rest of their lives. It didn't bear thinking about.

'Well, Eugenia?'

She found her voice, surprisingly calm and steady. 'I'll talk to Humphrey.'

'Is your date with him so important?'

'It's not only him—it's his mother. We spend a weekend with her every month or so.'

Mr Grenfell allowed a small sound to escape from him and turned it immediately into a cough. 'And it's essential that you spend this particular weekend with her?'

'It's not essential, it's just that we've been doing it for ages—well, ever since we became engaged.'

He said bracingly: 'All the more reason to give it a

miss for once. We shall leave in three days' time, fly to Frankfurt and drive the rest of the way. We shall be in Heidelberg for at least one week. Uniform, of course, and whatever else you can cram into a small case. I'll pick you up after lunch.'

Eugenia eyed him thoughtfully. 'I haven't said I'll go.'

He bent suddenly and kissed her cheek. 'Of course you'll go, Eugenia.' He added, to spoil it: 'You're a good nurse, and like to do your duty.'

She said meekly, feeling unhappy: 'Very well, Mr Grenfell. Shall I go to the Office?'

'No, I've already dealt with all that.'

Indignation sent the colour flying into her cheeks. 'Well, I must say—settling it all before you've even asked me.'

He smiled suddenly and her heart lurched. 'I was sure you'd come.' He opened the door and added briskly: 'Now how about taking a look at Mrs Cross? I'm not too happy about her.'

He was the remotely polite consultant again, so she was all the more surprised when he said: 'Thank you, dear girl,' and kissed her for a second time.

She had arranged to meet Humphrey that evening and wished heartily that she hadn't. Still, he had to be told, and should she tell him too that she didn't want to marry him, or should she turn her back on a hopeless love for Gerard and accept the future with him? She still didn't know the answer when she met him.

They walked down the street to the café where they occasionally had a meal. They had finished it and were drinking their coffee when she told him.

Humphrey was coldly furious. 'I've never heard such nonsense! You're not indispensable, Eugenia, any nurse would do. Mother will be bitterly disappointed.'

'There's the patient to be considered,' said Eugenia in a carefully mild voice.

Humphrey's good looks were spoilt by his sneer. 'Rather bigheaded, aren't you, darling? Selfish too—deliberately disregarding my wishes—Mother's too.'

Eugenia felt rage bubbling up inside her. 'Selfish?' Her voice, which she had kept low, became a little shrill. 'Selfish? When I've been saving every penny, going without clothes and holidays, going to cheap restaurants?' Her indignant gaze swept round the tiny place they were in. 'And the cheapest seats when we went to a show—and that's not been often. Spending weekends with your mother, who doesn't like me anyway.' She paused for breath, glaring at him, almost in tears. 'It's no good, Humphrey, we're not suited. I can't go on like this any longer, saving to get married and never getting any nearer to it, and even if we ever got married we'd still go on saving, because it's become a habit—a new car, some new gadget we simply had to have, and then planning the exact amount we needed before I could have a baby! I'm sorry, Humphrey, I really am, but it's simply no good—I'd be a dreadful hindrance, and I'd be so unhappy I'd turn into a nagging wife.' She studied his surprised face across the table. 'Besides, I don't love you.'

She felt instant contrition the moment she had said it, because she must have hurt him. But apparently not. Humphrey said coldly: 'It seems I've had a lucky escape—you seemed such a suitable girl when we became engaged. I see now that Mother was right.'

Which, as far as Eugenia was concerned, was the last straw. She pulled his ring off her finger and pushed it across the table towards him. She said breathlessly: 'She'll be glad. I'm sorry if I've hurt your feelings, Humphrey. You'll meet someone else.'

She didn't wait to hear his reply. In the street, she almost ran back to St Clare's. She was going through the gate when the Bentley passed her going the opposite way. She hadn't seen it, she was too intent on getting to her room so that she could have a good howl. She wasn't aware of Mr Grenfell stopping the car, getting out and joining her, not until he put out a hand and slowed her headlong rush.

He didn't say anything, only turned her round to take a good look at her pale face. After a moment he said: 'Ah, I have it. Humphrey has given you up.'

She nodded, then shook her head. 'No—that is, I've given him up.'

'I'm not surprised,' commented Mr Grenfell placidly. 'You're not a girl to marry one of the Humphreys of this world.'

She looked up at him. 'Whatever do you mean?'

'You're in no state to discuss the matter now. Go and make yourself a pot of tea and have a good cry and go to bed.' He studied her washed-out face. 'Go home tomorrow and talk to your father,' and when she took a questioning look at him: 'You'll feel better once you've done so.'

He gave her a friendly little pat on the arm. 'Just for the moment you're the wrong side of the curtain; when you lift it you'll see how splendid everything is on the other side.'

He opened the door for her and pushed her ever so gently inside, waiting while she crossed the entrance hall towards the nurses' home. When she had gone through the door at the back of the hall, he turned on his heel and went back to the Bentley.

Eugenia was surprised to wake the next morning and discover that she had slept all night, and since there was never time to waste on thinking in the mornings, she dressed, did her face, which she expected to look wan and pale and which looked just the same as usual, and went to breakfast. She didn't eat much, but no one noticed; they were too busy plying her with questions about her trip to Heidelberg. 'You lucky creature,' said someone from across the table. 'The second time in as many months, and such a romantic place too!' And someone else asked: 'Is Miriam going too?'

Eugenia looked surprised. 'I don't know. There's no reason why she shouldn't, is there? I daresay Mr Grenfell will have some free time once he's operated.'

'What is it this time?'

'Oh, C.A. of lung. An elderly man—I don't know more than that.'

The ward was busy, mercifully, so she had no time to think of anything but her work. There was no sign of Humphrey, but she hadn't expected there to be, and when Mr Grenfell came in the afternoon to take another look at Mrs Cross, he was his usual self, only as he prepared to leave the ward he paused to say: 'I'll give you a ring tomorrow some time—put you in the picture about the patient.' He gave her a sharp look. 'You're going home this evening?'

'Yes, Mr Grenfell.'

He nodded as he left her.

Eugenia was astounded when her father showed no surprise at her news.

'Well, love, I've been expecting it for some time now. You and Humphrey were never meant for each other; I'm relieved that you discovered it in time. You feel sore and hurt, and I daresay he does too, but you'll be surprised how soon you'll get over it. Now tell me about this patient in Heidelberg, it sounds most interesting. There's a hospital there, of course?'

'I should think so, Father, though I don't know a

thing about it. Mr Grenfell said he'd ring me tomorrow and give me the details. I expect it will be pretty much the same as the other case in the Algarve.'

The twins came in then, demanding supper, and when Eugenia told them that she wasn't going to marry Humphrey, whooped for joy. She felt a little shocked, and still more shocked to find that she shared their feelings.

She had refused to think about Mr Grenfell. He was something she would have to get over in secret, only she wasn't sure if she would be able to do that. If she couldn't then she would have to find another job, where she would never see him again. The thought turned her pale. Perhaps it would be easier to go on working for him, even though he married Miriam? She brushed the thought aside; time enough to worry about that after going on this new case with him. She must remember to be at her most professional with him. Cool and friendly, if she could manage it. It would help enormously, of course, if Miriam were to go with them.

CHAPTER NINE

MR GRENFELL collected Eugenia from the hospital entrance exactly on time, and there was no Miriam with him. Trying to ignore the wave of delight at seeing him, she told herself that of course she never would have come with them. Mr Grenfell had told her once that Miriam took no interest in his work. Work, she reminded herself, and just you remember that's all it is, my girl. She wished him a serene good morning, gave him her bag, and got into the car. Beyond a few commonplace remarks about the splendid weather he had very little to say, which gave her the opportunity to go over the details of the case which he had told her about over the phone on the previous evening. Herr Wolfgang Sauer, sixtyish with a wife and grown-up children; he had had symptoms and signs for several months and had waited too long before going to his doctor, although there was a good chance that something could be done as long as it was done with haste and by someone who knew his job. Mr Grenfell had said this without conceit. But first he would have to consult with the family doctor, see the anaesthetist, arrange for Herr Sauer's admission to hospital, all of which could be done quickly enough in an emergency. Eugenia did a mental recap of her duties, and by then they were at Heathrow.

Exactly as on the previous occasion, Mr Grenfell shepherded her through to the departure lounge, gave her coffee and magazines and made sure that she had all she wanted. And once on the plane, he settled in the seat beside her and, rather to her surprise, took the latest thriller from his case and began to read. Which left her nothing to do but bury her head in a magazine.

They landed at Frankfurt and were met by a small solemn man and a gleaming black BMW 735I. The man greeted them with pleasure and great politeness, stowed their bags and addressed himself to Mr Grenfell. Eugenia, whose German was, to say the least, sparse, listened to Mr Grenfell dealing with the language as though he had spoken it all his life, and envied him.

'Less than an hour's drive,' he told her. 'About fifty miles and a splendid road. We'll get a glimpse of the Rhine from time to time, and there are several castles. You're not tired?'

'Not in the least.'

Even if she had been tired nothing would have made her miss the scenery they were passing through with such speed. Castles perched on vine-covered hilltops with small picturesque towns at their foot; she repeated their names after Mr Grenfell's meticulous direction— Bensheim, Heppenheim, Weinheim, each with castles perched high above them.

'If only I can remember it all,' she said. 'I must get a map . . .'

Mr Grenfell smiled. 'We're still a mile or so from Heidelberg, and I doubt if you'll have much opportunity to explore. I'm told Herr Sauer is a demanding patient.'

They took a road to the left presently and she saw Heidelberg for the first time, much larger than she had imagined it to be, with hills towering behind it. 'It's too far for you to see, but there's a splendid castle just behind the town,' he told her.

She turned to look at him. 'You've been here before?'

'Oh, yes. It's a university town, you know that, of

course—I spent a year here, studying German.' He added quietly. 'That was a long time ago.'

'But you've remembered your German,' she said quickly.

'It's useful—at seminars and councils and so on.'

They were almost in the town by now. The castle was visible, a vast ruin dominating the town's narrow streets and old houses. But they didn't stop in the town but crossed a bridge over the river Neckar.

'Theodor-Heuss Bridge,' Mr Grenfell told her briefly. 'Now we're on the Philosopher's Way. Look back— there's the old town, the castle and the river.'

It was a view worth looking at. Eugenia hoped she would have the time to explore a little. She turned back as the car swung through tall iron gates and into a well tended and very large garden. The house was imposing, several stories high, painted white and with a steep roof pierced by small dormer windows. They went up steps to its solid front door, which was opened as they reached it. The thin elderly man who stood there said something which Eugenia couldn't understand and ushered them into the hall, a gloomy apartment, hung with weapons and stuffed animals' heads; exactly what Eugenia had imagined she would find in such a house. The room they were shown into was almost as bad; dark brown and heavy brocade, equally dark pictures on its walls and a large quantity of doubtless priceless china in its glass-fronted cabinets. Eugenia sat herself down, avoiding Mr Grenfell's eye, and presently the door opened and a woman came in—Frau Sauer, short and plump and middle-aged, and just now upset.

She shook Mr Grenfell's hand and burst into speech, and when she paused for breath he said something soothing, then went on in English: 'May I introduce my nurse? Sister Smith, in whom I have the greatest confidence. We've worked together for more than three years.'

Frau Sauer took her hand and shook it vigorously. 'You do not know how very glad I am to see you,' she said in fluent, heavily accented English. 'We have nurses, of course, but I understand that Mr Grenfell wishes to work with someone who knows his ways. I have ordered tea for you—you like tea?—and then you will be shown your rooms and our own Doctor Schwarz will be here and you can see my husband.' She turned back to Mr Grenfell. 'He is very ill—I am in despair.'

He said very kindly: 'It's too early for despair, Frau Sauer. I hope we shall be able to change that.'

Tea came on a vast silver tray, with a heavy silver teapot and delicate cups. The three of them sat drinking it while Mr Grenfell asked questions. He asked them in English, so that by the time they had finished, Eugenia knew a good deal more about her patient.

Frau Sauer put down her cup at last. 'You will want to freshen yourselves. Karl shall show you your rooms.' And when the thin man came: 'Be in the hall in ten minutes, please, Eugenia,' said Mr Grenfell, and left her with a fresh-faced girl who led her up the overpowering staircase, along a corridor and into a large room furnished richly in dark oak and overstuffed chairs. The bed looked comfortable, though, and Eugenia, who hadn't slept well, wished very much that she could curl up on it for an hour.

She was in the hall with a minute to spare, her make-up renewed, her hair tidied, smelling very faintly of Madame Rochas and soap and water. She looked bandbox-fresh and ready for anything.

Mr Grenfell, coming soundlessly from the staircase behind her, studied her at his leisure with a gleam in his eyes, but all he said as he joined her was: 'Uniform when you unpack, Eugenia. I fancy we shall have to get down to it without any waste of time.'

He turned to greet the man coming into the hall with Frau Sauer. Someone he already knew, who called him Gerard and then shook her hand and gave her a friendly smile. 'Sister Smith, this is a pleasure. You are Mr Grenfell's right hand, are you not? You do not mind coming? It is much better that he has a nurse with whom he is familiar—you will assist at the operation?'

'I shall scrub for it, I expect.' She glanced at Mr Grenfell, who nodded slightly. 'I feel rather an interloper, but I expect it saves time—Mr Grenfell does have his own way of doing things.'

She blushed a little as she caught Mr Grenfell's amused eye. 'How nicely put,' he observed. 'Frau Sauer, may we go somewhere for a few minutes and hear what Doctor Schwarz has to say about your husband?' He added: 'You too, Eugenia.'

They were ushered into a small room off the hall and sat down round a carved table. The two men talked for some time and Eugenia listened, only speaking when she was required to do so. They might have been on the ward, she mused; Mr Grenfell had become remote and thoughtful, his mind bent on the problems ahead of him. Finally they had agreed upon their procedure and Mr Grenfell had addressed her. 'Nursing duties will be sorted out when we've seen Herr Sauer, Eugenia. I should like you to come with us now.'

The patient, enthroned in a massive bed in an enormous room with enormous furniture, was indeed an ill man. At one time he must have been stout and well built, but now he looked nothing much more than a bag of bones. But Eugenia knew that bags of bones were by no means hopeless cases, however awful they looked—the right treatment given in time and they filled out nicely and resumed their lives, perhaps not quite as energetically as formerly, but at least there was a future for them.

She stood quietly by while Doctor Schwarz introduced Mr Grenfell and, after a few minutes' talk, herself. Herr Sauer spoke English very well, he even cracked a joke: 'I was beginning to think of angels, but I see that they are here as well as in heaven.'

They all laughed a little, and Eugenia blushed and tried to look severe.

'She may look like an angel,' observed Mr Grenfell, 'but I can assure you she's a martinet in her own field. You'll be in very safe hands, Herr Sauer.'

And after that he got down to business. The examination took a long time and there were X-rays to study, all the various tests to discuss with Doctor Schwarz.

They left their patient presently and Eugenia was left to get to know the nurse who had been living in the house for the past week or so. Not young any more, but pleasant-faced and placid and able to speak some English. She seemed glad to see Eugenia, too, and told her with something of a twinkle that their patient was at times very difficult. 'Of course he is a sick man,' she conceded, 'but two nurses have left already. I hope you will stay at least until he has recovered from the operation.'

Eugenia assured her that she would. 'Anyway, I couldn't go even if I wanted to; you see, Mr Grenfell is used to me looking after his patients and I know more or less all he wants done.'

She changed into uniform presently and went with Schwester Bonn to settle Mr Sauer for the night, and when that was done she was asked to go to the small room off the hall where Mr Grenfell was waiting for her.

'I'm going to operate at eight o'clock the day after tomorrow, so get all the prepping done, will you? I shall want you in Theatre. We'll go down to the hospital in the morning and you can meet everyone. Mr Sauer will stay in hospital for four or five days, perhaps longer, then come back here with two nurses—one of them will be you, of course. Be ready to stay for two weeks, Eugenia. A third nurse will join you for the second week so that you can phase out gradually. Anything you want to know?'

She shook her head. 'No, thank you—oh, yes. When will Mr Sauer go to the hospital?'

'Tomorrow afternoon, and you with him, of course. That should give you time to make sure you have everything you may need. Oh, and check my instruments over, will you?'

'Very well, Mr Grenfell. At what time do you want to take me to the hospital in the morning?'

'Nine o'clock.' He smiled at her and her heart turned over. 'Worried?'

'No, not at all. At least, I shall be if I can't make myself understood.'

'Don't worry, everyone on the case speaks English.'

Eugenia spent the rest of the evening going over the case with Schwester Bonn, got up early to attend to her patient's wants, and presented herself exactly at nine o'clock, spick and span in her uniform, in the hall where Mr Grenfell was waiting.

The hospital was modern and well equipped. She was taken to Theatre and allowed to roam around, getting to know where everything was, while Mr Grenfell talked to the anaesthetist and Theatre Sister.

'You don't mind me taking over?' ventured Eugenia when the men went away and left them together.

'No, not at all, Sister Smith . . .'

'Call me Eugenia, please.'

'Eugenia. It saves much time and temper if the surgeon has his own nurse with him, otherwise much time is lost explaining—and in another language too. There is a room ready for you, and we hope that you will be happy with us.'

Eugenia beamed at her. 'Oh, I shall, though I'll be busy for a day or two. Who have I got to help me?'

She went back with Mr Grenfell, satisfied that everything that could have been done to make the operation a success had been dealt with.

The rest of the day was taken up with preparations for the following morning and she didn't see Mr Grenfell again, nor, for that matter, Frau Sauer, as she and Schwester Bonn had their meals brought to them in a small room leading off their patient's bedroom. And the following morning she needed all her wits about her. Herr Sauer, ill though he was, made everything as difficult as possible, and she heaved a sigh of relief when he was stowed in the ambulance and she beside him.

It was still very early. She had done all she could at his home, but at the hospital there were still a number of tasks to do before eight o'clock. At a quarter to the hour she left him in Schwester Bonn's hands, and went to the theatre wing to scrub. The theatre had been readied, but there were still Mr Grenfell's own instruments to set out. She had arranged the last of these to her liking when the door opened and the patient was wheeled in, and a few minutes later Mr Grenfell, flanked by his assistants, came in.

The operation was a success, something she had never doubted. When it was over she divested herself of her theatre gown and cap and went along to her patient's room to take over from Schwester Bonn.

There was still a long way to go till the end of the day, but she wasn't in the least tired; there was too much to do.

She set about her tasks serenely, confident and meticulous. When Mr Grenfell joined her she handed him the chart and the observation sheets, then went to stand beside him as he bent over his patient.

He straightened up presently. 'So far so good. I want to know of any change immediately, Eugenia. You're prepared to stay until late this evening?'

'Yes, Mr Grenfell. How can I reach you?'

'I'll be here. You're sleeping here, of course?'

'Yes, they'll call me if I'm needed. Will Frau Sauer be visiting?'

'Not until this evening.' He nodded and went away, to reappear at intervals during the day.

Herr Sauer was tough. Towards evening, conscious for a short space, he said in a wispy voice: 'How long do I have to put up with these tubes?' He frowned. 'And this oxygen . . .'

'A day or so,' said Eugenia soothingly. 'They're important to your recovery, so bear with them.'

With the help of a nurse, she had sat him up against his pillows. 'Would you like a drink?'

He had had his drink and another injection and slept again until his wife slipped in with Mr Grenfell behind her. He opened his eyes then and smiled at her. 'I'll be home in a few days,' he told her.

And he was. Eugenia, making him comfortable in a chair in his bedroom, thanked heaven fervently that his recovery had been so uneventful; none of the complications which might have occurred had reared their ugly heads. True, he had been one of the worst patients she had ever had to deal with; irascible, finicky with his food, refusing to have certain nurses to attend to him, so that she found herself doing long hours. But it had been worth it. Here he was, back home, and with Schwester Bonn installed to share duties with her she could hope for a little leisure. There were still four days before the stitches were to be taken out, presumably they would return home shortly after that. She fetched his books and papers and put the telephone where he could reach it, then sat down at the table in one of the windows to bring her charts up to date. She had just finished when Mr Grenfell came in. She had seen him every day, of course, but never to talk to, only to receive instructions and give him reports on the patient, but now, when he had studied the papers she handed him, he paused.

'You've had a tough few days,' he observed. 'Herr Sauer is fit to be left with Schwester Bonn for a few hours. Take the morning duty, and see that you're free at noon for the rest of the day.'

Eugenia lifted tired eyes to his. 'Well, I would like that very much if no one minds. They were awfully good at the hospital; I got out most days for an hour.'

'I know, we'll be here for several days. I phoned your father during the week.'

'You did?' She smiled widely at him. 'How kind of you! I told him I'd be too busy to write.'

Mr Grenfell nodded. 'He sent his love, so did the twins.' He turned away. 'Frau Sauer wants to sit for an hour or so with her husband—he's rested enough?'

'Yes. They'll want to be alone?'

'Yes. The gardens are charming if you want a stroll without going too far.' He nodded briefly as he went.

Eugenia told Herr Sauer later on about her half day, and he patted her hand and said gruffly: 'Yes, Mr Grenfell told me, you deserve it, Eugenia. We're grateful, my wife and I. Enjoy yourself. Go to the Castle—it's worth a visit, perhaps more than one.'

Schwester Bonn came on duty very punctually. Eugenia was in her room by midday, tearing out of uniform, showering and getting into a cotton jersey dress. It was a gorgeous day, and she couldn't wait to get out into the sun. Lunch could wait; she would find a café somewhere and have a sandwich. She slung her bag over her shoulder and hurried downstairs. She was crossing the hall when Frau Sauer came out of the dining room. 'You will have a beautiful day, I hope. When you come back, ask for anything you want; Karl will attend to it.'

Eugenia thanked her politely. She intended to stay out just as long as possible, but perhaps she might be glad of coffee when she got back. She tried not to look too eager as she went through the door and down the steps. Mr Grenfell was sitting on the bottom one. He got up as she came to a halt beside him.

'I thought we might go up to the Castle. There's a restaurant just outside the gates, we can have something to eat and then explore. I've been lent a car.'

'Have you?' asked Eugenia faintly. 'How nice. But I'm quite all right on my own——'

'You've said that before, or don't you remember? Besides, I want to talk to you.' He marched her across the gravel sweep to a BMW sports coupé and shoved her gently into it. 'It's not far,' he observed as he got in beside her.

It was a very brief drive; he parked the car and ushered her into the restaurant, translated the menu and then sat back in his chair.

'You'll be glad to get back to St Clare's?' he asked idly.

'No,' said Eugenia baldly. 'I think—I'm almost sure that I'll leave St Clare's.'

Mr Grenfell took a pull at his lager. 'That sounds like a sensible idea. Any plans?'

She said woodenly: 'None—I daresay I'll think of something.' A pity she couldn't think of anything else to say, but he didn't appear to notice. They talked about their patient after that, a nice safe topic which took them through lunch and out into the sunshine again.

'Down here,' said Mr Grenfell, leaving the car where it was and starting to walk down a narrow lane and in through wide gates.

Just for a little while Eugenia forgot that she was unhappy; there was so much to see and he was the perfect companion. 'We won't try to see everything today,' he said, 'but there's something that might interest you.'

They went past a large stone arch, and when Eugenia paused to look at it, she was told it had been built in one night as a birthday present from Elector Friedrich the Fifth for his wife, Elizabeth Stuart.

'He must have loved her,' she observed, 'although a gate seems overdoing it a bit.'

'You would rather have pearls or a sable wrap?'

'Heavens, no—if someone loves you a bunch of roses would be ample proof.'

'I must remember that. This tower is called Dicker Turm.' He walked her past that, past what had once been the kitchens, past a vast frontage almost destroyed by lightning and still used for exhibitions, and then through an open door. They were in a chapel, its walls covered by various arms, a magnificent altar at its end.

'Beautiful, isn't it?' asked Mr Grenfell. 'You may not know that anyone who wishes can be married here. One merely arranges with the appropriate clergy, pays a fee of a hundred and fifty pounds and—er—ties the matrimonial knot.'

He had spoken casually, but his eyes were intent on her face.

Eugenia, who had stifled so many daydreams while she had been engaged to Humphrey, was having one at that very moment; arm in arm with Gerard, walking down the aisle towards a shadowy figure in clerical robes. She was roused from it by Mr Grenfell's voice. 'You like the idea?'

'Yes, oh, yes . . .'

'Tulle and roses and bridesmaids?' He sounded mocking and she said hastily:

'They don't matter . . .'

'But if you'd married Humphrey they would have mattered.'

She flushed a little. 'Yes—at least his mother expected . . .'

He made an impatient sound and she walked away from him, down the aisle towards the altar. 'All wood,' said Mr Grenfell, 'magnificently painted,' and then: 'You're silent. Why?'

She was looking away from him. 'I was thinking about the people who marry here.'

'And wishing you were one of them.' His tone was sharp.

'Well, I daresay most girls would—girls are romantic, you know.'

'And so,' said Mr Grenfell deliberately, 'are men, believe it or not! I'm of the opinion that when a man loves a woman he'll do his utmost to make her happy.'

He must be thinking of Miriam, she thought wistfully, although it was difficult to imagine him being besotted by anyone, but then she really didn't know him very well. At least, she knew him through and through because she loved him, but that was a different sort of knowing. She glanced at him and the expression on his face made her ask: 'Why do you look like that?'

'Like what?'

'Smug! As though you'd thought of something nice.'

'Nice, nice—what an inadequate word, rather let's say shatteringly delightful!

It seemed unlikely, just looking at his bland face, but perhaps he was having daydreams too about Miriam. She ventured timidly, quite unlike her usual calm self. 'Perhaps you would like to get married here?'

'That,' he said, still smug, 'is exactly what I have in mind.' He took her arm. 'Let's explore further.'

They wandered round, gazing at the Queen's House, the library, the Chemist's Tower, the Gate Tower, peering at stone statues and beautiful stonework and presently going down to the cellars to climb up and around the largest vat in the world.

'The grounds,' declared Mr Grenfell, 'are not to be missed.' He strode off, taking Eugenia with him, and she duly admired the splendid view from the terrace. 'You're not bored?' he asked her suddenly.

'Good gracious, no, I've never had such a marvellous day.'

'Good. We'll go back to the car and drive up to the restaurant at the top of the hill.' He gave her time to buy picture postcards on their way up the lane and lent her his pen so that she could write them and post them at once. She made her messages very brief in case he got impatient.

At the car she paused. 'Shouldn't I be getting back?' she asked.

'No, there's a nurse coming to relieve Schwester Bonn for the night. You'll go on duty again at seven o'clock tomorrow morning.'

'I wasn't told,' she began haughtily.

He stuffed her into the car. 'No need. Anyway, I've told you now, haven't I?

The view from the balcony of the restaurant was superb; their table was at its edge and Eugenia leaned her elbows on the balustrade and looked her fill. The wooded country sloped away towards the castle and the town below and then rose again in the distance. She said: 'I expect you travel quite a bit . . .'

'Indeed, yes, I can hardly avoid it. You like it here?'

'Yes, very much. Now that Herr Sauer is convalescing and I can have off duty I intend to explore.'

'There's a great deal more of the Castle to see.'

'I'll find time to come again.' She poured their tea and looked askance at the enormous chocolate and cream confection put before her.

'When in Rome . . .' advised Mr Grenfell. 'The Germans have a great liking for rich cakes.'

So they ate their cakes and talked about nothing much, and presently he said: 'There are some pleasant walks about here. Shall we try one?'

They strolled along in companionable silence, occasionally making desultory conversation, until Eugenia said uneasily: 'I really ought to go back.' She glanced at her watch. 'It's past six.'

'Don't fuss. Are you bored with my company?'

'Certainly not, it's—I—that is . . .' She stopped herself from saying what she longed to say.

Mr Grenfell seemed to find her muddled reply quite satisfactory. 'Good. Let's walk back and have dinner, then.'

They dined in the restaurant, already half filled, at a table by the window, its pink-shaded candle casting a charming glow over Eugenia's face. She was unaware of what she ate, just for a time she was a happy girl; no future, no past, just the wonderful present. They lingered over the meal; it was past nine o'clock by the time they left the restaurant and strolled to where the car was parked. It was still gloaming and they paused to watch the lights of Heidelberg far below and the faint glint of the river.

Mr Grenfell tucked an arm in hers. 'Blissful, isn't it? We must come again some time.'

He meant Miriam, of course. She said: 'I should think she—your fiancée would love it.'

'Miriam.' He spoke the name as though he had forgotten to whom it belonged. 'I took a leaf from your book—we're not getting married.'

Her heart gave a great leap and stuck in her throat so that her voice came out in a squeaking whisper. 'I'm sorry—she's so lovely.'

He said mildly: 'Yes, but there are others ... she intends to marry an American Tycoon. We'd outlived our romance if you could ever call it that.' He looked down at her. 'I intend to get married very soon.'

Eugenia stared at the twinkling lights of the town. 'I hope you'll be very happy.' She made a great effort and smiled at him in the dusk, glad that he couldn't see her face clearly. 'You should consider marrying in the Castle chapel.'

'I have, and we shall.'

She longed to ask him about the girl he was going to marry as they drove back; it would turn the knife in the wound and she couldn't frame the words. Instead she talked about the Castle and the scenery, and when they reached Herr Sauer's house, she got out quickly.

'It's been a lovely day,' she told him in a serene voice which gave nothing away. 'Thank you very much, Mr Grenfell.'

'Gerard.'

'Oh, well, Gerard,' she smiled. 'Goodnight.'

He didn't answer, but stretched out an arm and pulled her close and kissed her. And she kissed him back. She burned with shame thinking about it afterwards; not only had she kissed him, she had put her arms round his neck for good measure. She spent a dreadful night wondering how she would be able to face him in the morning.

But apparently he had forgotten all about it. He greeted her with his usual calm, exchanged the time of day with her and his patient, pronounced the latter to be well on the way to recovery and had then gone to talk to Schwester Bonn about her duties after he had left. Dr Schwarz came in shortly afterwards and they went away together, back to the hospital to check on previous X-rays of their patient. Eugenia, fresh and serene in her uniform, heaved a sigh of relief and fought a strong desire to burst into tears.

She went off duty for an hour or two in the afternoon and elected to go without her lunch, mainly because Mr Grenfell would be there. She shopped busily for presents to take home and when she got back discovered that he had paid his second visit to Herr Sauer and gone back to the hospital to have dinner with the anaesthetist and surgeon who had assisted him.

And the next morning he told her that they would be leaving on the following evening. 'So go over everything with Schwester Bonn, will you? I'll take the stitches out this evening, so have things ready for six o'clock.'

He went away and she didn't see him until he came in the evening, took out the stitches and then sat down to talk to his patient. Eugenia cleared up, carried the tray to the bathroom set aside for her use, and stayed there cleaning and sterilising forceps and scissors until she heard the door in her patient's room close.

She shared the morning chores with Schwester Bonn and then went off duty. She was putting things halfheartedly in her case when Mr Grenfell thumped on the door, and when she opened it: 'I thought we might have a quick drive round—we don't go until the late afternoon.'

'I'm packing.'

He glanced over her shoulder. 'Five minutes' work,' he opined briskly. 'You can spare an hour?'

Eugenia longed to go with him, but hesitated, by this time tomorrow they would be back at St Clare's and they might just as well be going to opposite ends of the earth. 'I'll be ready in ten minutes,' she said quietly.

She could taste her bitter disappointment when she reached the front door; there were two cars there and Gerard was talking to Frau Sauer and, most strangely, the Reverend Mr Pitt, the chaplain who took C. of E. services in one of the town's churches. She had met him while she had been at the hospital and had liked him; all the same, she wished him and Frau Sauer on the other side of the world. There was someone else there too; Herr Sauer's son, a solemn youngish man who shook hands gravely and stared at her hard.

'In you get,' said Mr Grenfell, and urged her into the car he had used previously. 'The others will follow us.'

'Oh, are they coming too?' Eugenia did her best to sound enthusiastic.

'I invited them,' he grinned wickedly, and just for a moment looked like a small boy up to mischief.

She supposed they were going somewhere for coffee or even lunch—a kind of farewell party, but instead of turning down to the town, they went up the hill towards the Castle. 'Don't you want to know where we're going?' asked Mr Grenfell.

She shook her head and lapsed into silence until

suddenly, halfway round a hairpin bend, Mr Grenfell spoke. 'There's something about which I have to know.' His voice was so urgent that she turned her head to look at him. 'Have you quite recovered from Humphrey?—and don't, I beg of you, tell me that it's none of my business.'

'Well, actually it isn't.' She spoke with a touch of her old spirit. 'But if you must know—well, yes, I have.'

He didn't answer, only swung the car into the car park, opened her door and stood waiting with her until the others joined them.

Coffee in the Castle restaurant, guessed Eugenia, and joined up with the Reverend Mr Pitt, and then Dr Schwarz stopped with a squeal of brakes and leapt out to join Mr Grenfell.

They made their way unhurriedly, past the Dicker Turm and the Winter Queen's Gate, and then down steps and through a low doorway and on through a narrow rough-hewn passage into the King's Chamber. Eugenia hadn't been there, and she listened politely to her companion prosing on about the various portraits of successive Electors hanging on its walls. He was still only halfway through the family history as they mounted a couple of steps and entered the adjoining apartment, vast and sparsely furnished and with a great porcelain stove in one corner; she wasn't sure when Mr Pitt was no longer beside her. Mr Grenfell was there instead, engulfing her hand in his large reassuring clasp, whisking her ahead of the rest of the party, into the next enormous room and towards a circular stone staircase. On its step, the top one, he paused; there was no one else behind them. The others were still lingering in the first room. Eugenia looked at him enquiringly, and gave a little gasp at what she saw in his face.

'You kissed me, my darling. I've been waiting for

that. I think I've always been in love with you, only I didn't know it, and when I did there were so many good reasons for not telling you . . .'

'Such as?' asked Eugenia softly.

'I'm not as young as I was, I'm bad-tempered, irascible, impatient—but never with you, my darling. I think we might live very happily together. I promise you I'll be a good husband and a doting father.'

'If you must know,' said Eugenia, 'I think you're the most wonderful man on this earth. I've been . . .' She blinked away tears. 'I thought you said you were going to get married . . .'

He bent to kiss her slowly. 'And so I am—to you, sweetheart. Why else should we be here?'

She opened her lovely eyes wide. 'Here? Now? I'm not dressed . . .'

He smiled and kissed her once more. 'My love, Mr Pitt is here to marry us and the others will be witnesses to our wedding. You wanted to be married here, you said that roses would do instead of mink. Well, the roses are waiting, and so is Mr Pitt.'

Eugenia took a deep breath.

'We mustn't keep them waiting, Gerard. What about going back to England?'

'I cancelled the flight tickets. We'll have a few days here—together. I'm borrowing the car and we'll drive through the Black Forest.'

'I've no clothes . . .'

'You said that just now, my darling. We'll buy what you need as we go.'

Just for a moment she had a vivid picture of Humphrey saying that, and laughter bubbled up inside her. 'Oh, we're going to be so happy,' she told him.

He didn't say anything, only smiled so that her insides melted, then took her hand and walked down the staircase and into the chapel. The others were there; waiting on a bench by the door was a bouquet of roses.

Mr Grenfell picked them up and put them in her hands. 'I forgot to ask you if you'll marry me, Eugenia,' he said.

She smiled at him, sniffing at the fragrant flowers. 'Yes, Gerard, I will—most certainly I will!'

Harlequin Romance

THE LEO MAN

Harlequin Romance

THE WINDS of Winter
Sandra Field

Harlequin Romance

Love Beyond Reason

Harlequin Romance

Man of Power
Mary Wibberley

4
FREE
Harlequin Romances

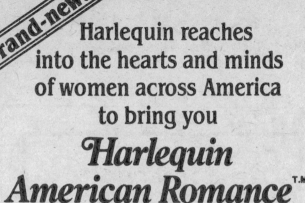

NOW! Your chance to receive all these books in this exciting new series the moment they come off the presses!

Mail to:
Harlequin Reader Service

In the U.S.
2504 West Southern Ave.
Tempe, AZ 85282

In Canada
P.O. Box 2800, Postal Station A
5170 Yonge St., Willowdale, Ont. M2N 6J3

YES! I want to be one of the first to discover the new **Harlequin American Romance** novels. Please send me the 4 new **Harlequin American Romance** novels each month as soon as they come off the presses. I understand that I will be billed only $2.25 for each book (total $9.00). There are no shipping or handling charges. There is no minimum number of books that I have to purchase. In fact, I may cancel this arrangement at any time.

154 BPA NAZE

Name   (please print)

Address   Apt. no.

City   State/Prov.   Zip/Postal Code

Signature (If under 18, parent or guardian must sign.)

AMR-SUB-3X